PENGUIN BOOKS

CHILD'S PLAY

David Malouf was born in Brisbane. His father's family came to Australia from Lebanon in the 1880s and his mother's family from London just before the First World War. He was educated at the Brisbane Grammar School and the University of Queensland.

His many awards include the NSW Premier's Award for Fiction for *An Imaginary Life*, the 1982 Melbourne *Age* Book of the Year Award for *Fly Away Peter* (Penguin 1983), and the Gold Medal of the Australian Literature Society for *Neighbours in a Thicket*, a collection of poems, in 1974, and again in 1983 for *Child's Play* and *Fly Away Peter*. In 1985 *Antipodes* was awarded the Vance Palmer Award for Fiction. *Voss*, an opera from the novel of Patrick White with libretto by David Malouf and music by Richard Meale, was first performed in Adelaide in 1986 by the Australian Opera and has since been recorded.

In 1988 he was the first winner of the Pascall Prize for achievement of excellence in creative writing.

Other books by David Malouf

FICTION

Johnno (1975)
An Imaginary Life (1978)
Fly Away Peter (1982)
Harland's Half Acre (1984)
Antipodes (1985)

POETRY

'Interiors' in *Four Poets* (1962)
Bicycle and Other Poems (1969)
Neighbours in a Thicket (1974)
The Year of the Foxes and Other Poems (1979)
First Things Last (1980)
Wild Lemons (1981)

ESSAYS

12 Edmondstone Street (1986)

CHILD'S PLAY

WITH
EUSTACE
AND
THE PROWLER

DAVID MALOUF

PENGUIN BOOKS

Penguin Books Australia Ltd
487 Maroondah Highway, PO Box 257
Ringwood, Victoria, 3134, Australia
Penguin Books Ltd
Harmondsworth, Middlesex, England
Viking Penguin, A Division of Penguin Books USA Inc.
375 Hudson Street, New York, New York 10014, USA
Penguin Books Canada Limited
10 Alcorn Avenue, Toronto, Ontario, Canada M4V 1E4
Penguin Books (N.Z.) Ltd
182-190 Wairau Road, Auckland 10, New Zealand

First published by Chatto & Windus Ltd, 1982
Published by Penguin Books Australia, 1983
6 8 10 9 7 5
Copyright © David Malouf, 1982

Offset from the Chatto & Windus hardback edition
Made and printed in Australia by The Book Printer

National Library of Australia
Cataloguing-in-Publication data:

Malouf, David, 1934
Child's play
ISBN 0 14 007016 8
I. Title
A823'.3

CONTENTS

CHILD'S PLAY   1

EUSTACE   147

THE PROWLER   179

CHILD'S PLAY

1

One afternoon at the end of autumn, during my last time at home with my father – a farewell visit is how I thought of it, though with any luck it might not be – I walked alone to an abandoned farmhouse on the other side of the stream that was up for sale at last and which I thought I might make a bid for; a way perhaps of ensuring the future would exist by setting my hand to an official document, a ninety-nine year lease.

I had known the place as a child and always loved it. It stands on a slight rise looking back into the valley, an unusual view that suggests that before there was a farm there the site might have had other, darker uses. Two ancient cherry-trees grow hard against the wall, there are pears, apples, half-a-dozen stunted olives; but what always attracted me to the place were the markings on its marble doorstep. A single stone, deep sunk and hollowed with footsteps, it might once, my father suggested, have been an Etruscan altar.

It was a clear day without cloud and unseasonably warm, which I took to be, on the sky's part, a special dispensation in my favour, a kind of blessing. I undressed, waded waist deep in the icy stream, stretched out afterwards on the gravel shore till I was dry enough to resume my clothes, and began the climb uphill, through thickets of tangled broom and deep, thickset brambles. It took nearly an hour.

The doorstep was smaller than I had remembered, but the markings, two rows of them, were still there, cut so deep you could read them with your fingers, and I had the sudden clear recollection in doing so in the bright sunlight of the first time I had tried it as a child. The script, my father insisted, was indecipherable. But I had been convinced that the stone stood in a unique relationship to me and that if I shut my eyes and traced the letters with my fingers the darkness itself would reveal their meaning. The idea now made me smile. But I shut my eyes just the same and my fingers followed the grooves.

The key was where the agent said it would be, tucked into a crack between bricks. Slapping the big roan mare that had followed me up from the gate and stood nuzzling my palm, I stepped through into the ground-floor stall. The horse, smelling apples, poked her soft nose in after me.

I had come here often as a child – the place had been deserted for as long as I could remember – but only in summer when the stream was low enough to be crossed dry-shod. Exploring the high rooms had been one of my first adventures. Then later, as a lonely adolescent, I had come to read or daydream and to try, once again, with pen and paper, to solve the mystery of the Etruscan writing. There were two rooms overhead and an attic. Down below a feeding trough ran the length of the wall, with iron rings every metre or so where the cattle were tethered. There was straw, a bundle of kindling, the rich ammoniac smell of animal droppings.

I climbed the stairs. Several tiles were missing from the low-pitched roof and the woodwork, thin slats with tiles laid over them, showed through jagged gaps. The whole place was filled with a subdued autumn light that smelled intensely of apples, and in the second and larger room there was a spilled heap of them, wrinkled now and some of them wizened to the size of walnuts but still deliciously sweet. I sat on the stone floor and munched away as if I hadn't eaten for a week, swallowing each apple whole, with real greed, then reaching for another. It was like biting into the sun. Down below the horse rubbed her flanks against the door jamb and stamped her foot on the earth.

Stretched out there in the familiar warmth under the roof, I felt transparent, filled with the breath of apples, biting into the future with absolute certainty now that it would be there, that I would survive my moment in the Piazza Sant' Agostino at P. and come back, and had no need to buy a house or do anything else to ensure it; that I would live for years, maybe for ever. It is difficult to explain these convictions without seeming foolish. They come to us from deep within, even if we receive the ambiguous message as a smell of apples, the gold of a late autumn afternoon, the taste, as we put it, of the sun.

3

But I should introduce myself.

I am twenty-nine years old and male. You will understand if I decline to give further particulars.

I am what the newspapers call a terrorist.

2

I have been living for nearly six weeks in a small, one-roomed apartment in the Palazzo C, just the sort of place – bedroom not much bigger than a cupboard, with a gasring for making coffee and a washbasin behind a screen – that lone students inhabit or workmen who have come in from the country.

There are a dozen of us on the fourth floor across the courtyard, all living in spaces created out of what must once have been servants' quarters, modest enough by the standards of an earlier century and now even further divided. It is a rats' nest.

Narrow stairways branch off into darkness at every turning. One of them must pass just behind my bed. I wake sometimes to hear footsteps, not twenty centimetres from my ear. It is as if someone were climbing, seven steps in all, into my skull. Another crosses the corner of the ceiling opposite. I have no clear picture of how the rooms and passageways in this part of the building are connected or where my room sits among them. I know the courtyard and a stone stairway leading out of it, a passage and its turnings, another stairway, another, a third even narrower than the last, then my door. It is better like that. Once I have reached the second floor I am beyond the point where I am likely to come face to face with anyone, either by night or by day.

The palace dates from the Renaissance and is still inhabited somewhere by the family of the duke. They must live in the *piano nobile* on the other side of the courtyard; I have on occasion seen lights in the big windows above the square. The second floor on that side is offices, lawyers for the most part with the usual medley of clients, and the third houses a language school whose students, full of noisy high spirits, crowd the vestibule, hang about in groups on the stairs and are endlessly passing in and out of the barred carriage-way.

All this traffic means that the main door, which is three metres high and of solid walnut, is never shut. It also means that those who pass in and out go largely unremarked by the two porters. There are so many different types: separated couples and petty criminals in three-piece suits on their way to consult the lawyers, Swedish, American and English girls, Brazilians, New Zealanders, Swiss, sometimes a half-dozen Egyptians or an African army or police corps looking uncomfortably out of place as civilians, foreign executives, airline pilots, hippies – all students of the two-week course at the language school.

A single terrorist of quiet habits and with no distinguishing marks, heavy hair neither long nor short, jeans and Levi jacket some months faded, tallish,

6

middle to late twenties, would pass un-noticed among this gathering of the nations. Some of my neighbours on the fourth floor must be genuine workmen, but given that they too wear jeans and a Levi jacket, have moustaches, sideburns and are of quiet habits, they may equally be language students, or students of art or literature, or terrorists.

The courtyard is damp and all its walls are scarred and patched with damp. The arcades, closed off with ironwork screens of a depressing brutality and weight, are piled with firewood and broken stones, fragments of what must once have been noble decoration. The various classical deities, minus a flexed wrist or with the genitals amputated or half the face gone as in a stroke, rub shoulders with eagles, peacocks, cornucopias, flamelike finials, quartered shields and heraldic beasts both real and fabulous, urns, putti, wingless angels gone green with mould – an anthology, as it were, of our rarest follies and illusions.

The main staircase is barred with ironwork and never used. It bears a short chain, doubled, and a rusty padlock. All entrance to the apartments on the second and third floor, and to our wing at the rear, is by the same stone stairway in the corner of the yard.

I have seen lights in the windows at all levels in these side wings but have never met anyone on the stairway or glimpsed even a shadow in the various corridors.

Once, looking up briefly as I passed through the inner portal, I saw a hand watering a geranium pot and a puff of what must have been pipe smoke. On another occasion, late at night, I heard a thin male voice calling 'Lady, where are you Lady? Why won't you come to poppa? Poppa's lonely. Where are you?' I assume he was calling to one of the several cats, some wild, others no doubt domesticated, that stretch themselves on the warm flags of the courtyard or among the broken gods and putti behind the grills, and make their way precariously, between pots of geranium and petunia, from one side of the palace to the other, tracking the sun. On yet another occasion, turning the stairs at the second landing, I heard from a half-open door down one of the corridors, the sounds of a man and woman fighting. The woman uttered piercing screams, the man's voice murmured soft indistinguishable petitions, and the whole scrabbled din was punctuated by muffled thuds that must have been blows. Then before I was quite out of earshot, the whole episode concluded with the slamming of a door.

The room was found for me. I came straight to it from the station, having been in the city only once before, when my father brought me as a child to visit the museum. The name of the palace and the number of my room, with indications of how to find it, headed a list that includes four safe restaurants, four laundromats that are within easy walking distance (I never go to the same one twice) and three streets in different quarters where there are prostitutes.

All this is perfect. The palace, with its promiscuous entry and its world of obscure privacies, is cover. The city too is cover, crowded as it is at all times of the year with tourists, transient students of language, permanent students at the various art schools and technical colleges, and at the University. I am invisible here. I go out of my room at eight like any factory hand or office worker and return at dusk. In the evening I dine alone and go to a movie.

I am invisible. Just like everyone.

3

Our hideout as the newspapers would say (we call it an office) is in an apartment block on the other side of the river. I take two buses then go on foot for the last three hundred metres, through a maze of streets too narrow for traffic; under archways, down twisting lanes, across piazzas no bigger than a pocket handkerchief where women, in the pale sunlight of these April mornings, are already throwing buckets of water over the cobbles or setting up stalls with vegetables and cut flowers and men are at work delivering trays of pastry, crates of Fanta and Coca Cola and barrels of anchovies in brine.

Cut off as I have been over these last weeks from all the happenings of ordinary existence – I am by nature gregarious, not at all the brooding melancholic – I find the busy traffic of the quarter, with all its comings and goings, an endlessly engaging spectacle and take longer on my way to the office than the distance strictly demands. It makes up a little for the hours I spend alone in my barren room and for the narrow and impersonal view that is required by my work. Not that

I complain of this. It is necessary. It is a discipline. But it goes against the grain with me, and I find it easier to concentrate on pure facts if, for a few minutes before, I have been able to observe the confusion of voices and events that makes up the city and can retain, somewhere in the back of my head, the conviction that it is real and continuous and will be there to be re-entered when I am done. Each time I go down, with all the dossiers of my 'case' locked up in the filing cabinet behind me, is a rehearsal for my final re-emergence. For I have not relinquished life or given up even one of my high ambitions and hopes for the future. What I have given up is some weeks of my life and my legal innocence; and I have done so, I believe, in the name of that very life of the streets – ordinary, loud, richly confusing – that I shall go back to when my mission is complete.

Rich confusion is not its only quality, of course. There are patterns, and I find them sustaining. (Is my nature really conservative?)

I like for example to see the same children, at the same hour, making their way in noisy groups towards the primary schools across from the park; skipping along hand in hand, trudging with head lowered as they repeat some childish spell and try, without trying, not to step on the lines, dancing backward on their heels to call to a straggler. Their scrubbed faces shine. They have little satchels strapped to their backs, or carry brief-cases that are too big for them and drag their bodies awkwardly to one side. Bright blue pinafores cover their sweaters and slacks.

For all these weeks a team of plasterers has been at work on an old palazzo near my bus-stop, and usually, by the time I pass, they are already on the job, balanced high up on the iron scaffolding or on planks and ladders in the open rooms. They are a boisterous lot, forever shouting from room to room or calling into the street. Their heads are protected with linen caps, their overalls caked with plaster, and the youngest of them, the apprentice, is regularly covered from head to foot with the paint he has been mixing. I like to see them up there, busily swinging their brushes, joking and calling to one another, or pausing to watch a pretty girl pass in the street below, and have begun to reckon time by their progress up the side of the building and through its rooms, by the changing colours of what can be seen of the interior, all sparkling fresh with new paint and soon to be occupied. The work of these decorators, and the great corner palace itself, has become my private clock. I often consult it when I need to fix, in the otherwise featureless landscape of these weeks, some little event or movement of my own thoughts. *Ah yes,* I say, *that was before those rooms on the second floor had the gilt on their ceilings. Or was it after? Yes, after.*

Then there are the beggars, always the same ones; each quarter has its own.

An old woman bent almost double, who wears boots that are a size too large for her, has her own place near the paper stand. With one hand boldly extended and her face bent low to the pavement, she murmurs an incomprehensible litany. Further on a youth with a

12

shaven head sits hunched against the wall with his face between his knees. An empty box lies on the pavement beside him, together with a placard describing his plight: he is blind and has neither family nor work. Passers-by, always the same ones, dip their hands in their pockets or turn delicately aside (the women) to examine their purse. They place coins in the outstretched palm, or leaning over, drop them very discreetly into the box.

All this is part of the fabric of things and is essential to its pattern. So too is the fat owner of the hardware shop, who stands in the doorway under the hanging pots, pans, broomsticks, and the tin and plastic buckets, with a black book in her hand, always the same one, which I assume is a bible and which when the sun is shining she sits reading on a three-legged stool. And the delivery vans with their various boys; and the early shoppers with their plastic bags printed with the names of local stores. It is against the accommodations, the collisions, the dense proximities of this street life, all its repeated details and events, confused but not without shape, that the simplicity of my own existence should be balanced, with its single event that must, for a while yet, be held back and kept separate and made to occupy my whole mind, but will at last become part of that rich confusion and may even change it a little. That this event is a killing is neither here nor there. Violence too has its place. There are brawls, road accidents, beatings-up behind closed doors; or one of my decorators might suddenly miss his footing and fall twenty metres from the scaffolding. There is death. The important thing is not to see the single event in isolation. Though in fact, for these weeks, that is just how I am required to see it. And that is why, for the sake of my own sanity, I have to spend a little time each day in the street.

But I should return to the facts.

Our office.

It is housed in an apartment block that presents the same faded appearance, crumbling plaster, patches of raw brick, as every other building in this older part of the city. At street level there is a showroom for bathroom fittings, on the first floor an architect's office; beyond that a dozen big, comfortable apartments. Ours bears the name *Rizzoli, G.* on a brass plate in the vestibule, and on another, larger and more elaborate, in the middle of the door.

Inside, what ought to be a family dwelling has been set up as office, library, information-bank and arsenal. It is all very cleverly and professionally arranged.

Five of us work here from half-past eight in the morning till seven at night, six days of the week. We work in the big main room of the apartment, which can be sealed off and defended from the corridor. We each have a desk facing the wall and a filing-cabinet, and we are always armed. It is strange to sit all day, as you might sit in the corner of a quiet library, bringing your mind to bear on a set of problems or giving it free range in the fields of the imagination, and to have always at your side the weight, the coldness (till it absorbs a little of your own body-heat) of a revolver; and even stranger to know that you might, at any moment, have to use it. We have all been trained to use weapons and could fight our way out of here should it become necessary; or at least hold off an attack till our records were destroyed. The presence of cold steel is a reminder of our vulnerability and keeps us alert. It also keeps us aware, during these quiet library days among the facts and photographs, of that hard moment to which they lead, when we will stand alone at last with the weapon naked in our hand.

One of the bedrooms is a library and information bank that contains, for example, lists of prospective victims, their names, their addresses and the first essentials for a study of their life and habits.

The other, though still set up as a sleeping place, with double-bed, dressing-table and lace curtains in the window, is our arsenal. The built-in wardrobe is stocked with hand-grenades, revolvers of various weights and calibres, repeating pistols, machine guns, anti-tank missiles, dynamite sticks and other devices for the manufacture of bombs, and a good supply of ammunition. But the bed is changed and slept in, there are cosmetics on the dressing table, clothes in the wardrobe: woollen suits neatly covered with clear plastic oversheets, summer dresses, scarves, and on a shelf at the bottom a whole row of sensible shoes and (a little incongruously one might think) a pair of coral-pink glossy leather sandals. We must assume that Signora or Signorina Rizzoli, Gina, has a real existence and lives here in the hours when we are away. Along with the usual mail, two popular magazines are delivered in her name every second

15

Thursday – the sort that are devoted to the lives of starlets and to international gossip, together with a parish newsletter.

She fascinates me this Signora Rizzoli, who sees that the kitchen is supplied with the makings of a good lunch and whose grey hairs I have examined in a hairbrush but who herself remains mysteriously invisible. By the time we appear in the morning she has already left. We just miss her; though only, I suspect, by minutes. Have we passed in the street below without recognizing one another? Or was the ignorance on one side only? Does she perhaps keep watch on us, our appearance, our times of arrival and departure, and file a report?

It is in the nature of things that I have no answer to these questions. I know nothing of the structure of our organization and its agencies, or the part that might be played in it by a Signora Rizzoli. I have been recruited for a special purpose and my ties with the organization involve a single event, after which I shall sever all connection with it and disappear. Signora Rizzoli, like so much else that occupies me here, both fascinates and eludes me.

Those coral pink sandals for instance. It is part of my failure to catch and hold her – a failure that rather pleases me, I find it reassuring – that those sandals cannot be fitted to what I already know of her life and interests. Sitting there at the bottom of the wardrobe among her sensible shoes they seem deliberately intended to mislead. What do they represent? A secret weakness, a lapse in taste, a lapse of character? Some fleeting image of herself in the window of a boutique that she was unable to resist and keeps shamefully hidden from view? I imagine Signora Rizzoli, when no one else is here, taking her coral-pink sandals from the wardrobe, strapping them to her small feet, and walking round the apartment as if it were a fashionable summer beach, deliberately stepping out of character and using the sandals, as she uses the two magazines and the parish weekly, to throw off the scent an imaginary policemen who might already have his eye on the dour, dark-suited language teacher. Or are the sensible shoes, the pink sandals, the magazines, the parish weekly and the Signora's role as language teacher all of a piece? And is it precisely this that makes her, from the organization's point of view, the perfect owner-occupier of an apartment that is being used by terrorists?

While we are at our desks in the workroom, between half-past eight and twelve-thirty, and again between half-past one and seven, we are forbidden to speak, and though this rule does not apply to the dining room, we do not speak there either.

This self-imposed isolation, as of a religious order, has no ideology behind it for which the religious life would be a proper model; it grows out of our work. There is something excessive, comic even, about those nineteenth-century anarchists who thought of themselves as a new breed of monks, above life and its ordinary conditions, abjuring alcohol and women and even denying themselves tobacco. We are workers, technologists; young people of good health, clear of

17

spirit, and with no grudges, no phobias, no sense of personal injustice or injury, none of those psychological or physical defects that are so dear to the hearts of journalists and so comforting to their readers. If we keep to ourselves and eat in silence it is because we have, in our long hours at the desk, gone too deep into the future and stood too long, in imagination, in our lonely moment there, to indulge in small talk or the commonplaces of a social life. There are cells that are units, training together for a group event, a bank robbery or a raid on a rival organization. Others come together only out of administrative convenience and for mutual protection. Ours is of the second sort. We each have our separate commissions and work alone.

But there is another reason why we preserve a wary distance from one another and prefer to see no more than appears on the surface or can be guessed at from those little habits of behaviour and appearance that inevitably give one away.

What we bring to the office is a steely impersonality that belongs to our role as killers. It looks inviolable, and it must be so. It is a form of security. To open to others all that lies beyond the hard surface, the doubts, fears, hesitations, anxieties of the lonely individual, all the soft dark life within – those moments when, walking along in sunlight, you come suddenly to a full realization of what you have let yourself in for, the irreversible nightmare – would be to introduce an element that might entirely destroy us, since it is on a steady imperviousness to all this, to the need that grips you some days to speak out and share a moment of tenderness felt or poignantly recalled, an unimportant event out of a past that is dense with unimportant but memorable events, that our security is established. What makes us useful as killers is that we have no past. The crimes we are to commit have no continuity with us. Nothing in their geography, their politics, their psychology, leads back to what we are. To speak out and offer confidences, to exchange memories, would be entirely disruptive. So we say nothing, and of those others who make up the four remaining points of the pentagram I know only what I can see, or have picked up by intuition from what cannot, even with effort, be concealed.

Carla (it is not her real name, we all have code-names here) occupies the working-place behind me. She is a tall blond girl who wears expensive cardigans, tweed skirts, boots. She smokes incessantly with quick nervous movements like a non-smoker, sucking at the cigarette and pulling it quickly away from her mouth with a gesture that has to be carried through to arm's length, and when she laughs she shows all her teeth; it is as if she had convinced herself that laughing is good for the facial muscles and should be made the most of. She is the only one of us who looks a little, I think, like a fanatic.

When her face is in response she has a faintly disdainful air, as though there emanated from some object in her vicinity an odour of corruption that is just detectable to her finer nostrils. She is a perfectionist. I watch her lean over a page, and with an eraser held very precisely between thumb and fore-finger, remove an error. The tip of her tongue appears. The agent of her moral being, her tongue is very lively and pink; it moves with the eraser and is committed to silence. 'There,' she says, dealing gently with God, 'I have erased an error. I have erased one of *Your* errors. The page is blank again.' She lifts a strand of hair from her eyes and smiles with satisfaction, like a very competent twelve-year-old, but when she glances up and finds me looking her brow creases. I have caught her in a moment from the past.

At mealtimes she crumbles her bread nervously with her left hand and does not eat it – a habit I find un-nerving, I can't say why; and when she walks she strides. I think of her being pulled along at the end of a straining leash by some invisible hound. These are observations that may point to none of the conclusions I draw from them. Namely, that Carla is convent educated, country bred and a lapsed aristocrat. She is highly efficient in every way and cooks, when it is her turn, with the same swift sure movements with which she smokes, flips through file-cards and makes her way through a crowd. She is the one I would put my trust in if (it is one of those things we have to consider) there were a raid on the apartment and we had to shoot our way out.

I wonder sometimes about her *event*. I see her advancing through glass doors to a bank hold-up, her leather boots squeaking softly on the parquet floor. I imagine what it would be like to be an old man, full of the corruptions of thirty years in office, who looks up suddenly to find her there, tall, unsmiling, with a repeating pistol in her hand, one of our beautiful Scorpions, and recognizes, with what mixture I ask myself of terror, relief, a disturbed and gratifying sensuality, the cool angel of his extinction.

For some reason when we go dancing I never choose Carla as a partner.

The truth is that she intimidates me. What was she in her former life? A student of anthropology, the bored wife of a city lawyer, a make-up consultant for a beauty firm? She is twenty-eight or thirty and her right hand shows a band on the fourth finger where she previously wore a ring. Once she passed boldly, but fleetingly, through one of my dreams. I feel sometimes that her appearance there, and the glow she left on my senses, told me more of what she really is than all our hours of sitting side by side in the apartment, and more than I have been able to deduce from my observations of her behaviour. But that sort of knowledge is untranslatable. Does she, I wonder, detect the small changes it has made in my attitude to her? Far from leading to greater intimacy between us it has put me at a disadvantage. She seems, more than ever, a mystery that I will never solve.

Antonella is a South American, from Chile or Uruguay. She wears an embroidered cloak, but is really too short to carry it off, and is so full of energy that even when she is working, absorbed in her files, or brooding, with a glass screwed into her eye, over a strip of tiny photographs, she suggests a girl dancing, moving about in her secret self to some popular song that she is humming under her breath, or maybe

21

whistling – I see her as a whistler. It is a notion so strong in my sense of her that I find myself being distracted by her singing, and am tempted at times to turn round in the absolute silence and say, 'Antonella, for heaven's sake, be quiet! I can't work for the racket you're making.' Even at the dinner-table she sits in something less than silence. Like a bottle that is bubbling and about to pop its cork.

She cannot be more than twenty. I think of her as the eldest of a family of three or four. She gives the impression of a girl who has just (I say just but it may be weeks ago) wished an exuberant farewell to smaller brothers and a sister, and is still full of the glow of their affection for her and their sorrow to see her gone; as if, perhaps, she had slipped in to kiss the youngest of them in the bath and in leaning over the tub got soap bubbles in her hair that have not yet evaporated. She dances well, cooks badly, and is efficient in everything to do with her work; mostly, one suspects, because she is naturally careless and has to watch herself. If any one of us were to indulge in a practical joke it would be Antonella – though I can't imagine what form it might take. Strangely enough, she and Carla, for all their difference, get on enormously well. We are forbidden to see one another outside, except for the special occasions when we go dancing, but inside the apartment, in all sorts of small ways, one feels them moving together; whereas we males, less sure of ourselves, practice a wary hostility.

I can understand this in Enzo's case. He is a natural leader who finds himself now in a situation where all

22

that side of him is superfluous because no leader is required.

It is comic to watch Enzo struggle with himself, to see him exclude from our relations with one another everything that is strongest in him. Comic, but also endearing. (Why are men so much more transparent than women? Is it because so large a part of what we are has to be recognized and appreciated by others?) Enzo's dark good looks, his marvellous head of hair, which he cannot prevent himself from tossing, his air of being a swimming star or a skier out of season, his obvious appeal to women, his confidence in his own power and presence – these are difficult qualities to exclude, and one has the sense of their waiting there, a little impatiently, a little petulantly, to be called back into the room and given full play among us. His hostility to Arturo and me is less, I think, because of any threat we present to his supremacy than for the hurt he feels on behalf of his banished 'qualities'. As if otherwise we might fail to appreciate that equality has been established among us only because of his noble abnegation.

Arturo's hostility on the other hand is defensive. He is a stocky nineteen-year-old with a mop of tight, blondish curls, strong, hard-working, good-humoured and afraid of being ignored because of his youth. It makes him hard-mouthed and aggressive on occasion, and more boyish than ever.

Once, by some unlucky accident, I ran into him at a pornographic movie. He was fiercely embarrassed. Here we are training together in the technology of murder and he is embarrassed to be seen at a porno movie. Our eyes met and he blushed and looked away, as if somewhere behind me stood the respectable peasants of the village he comes from, all dressed in their Sunday suits, rattling their watch-chains and saying, But that's Ivo's boy. He's been watching a dirty movie.'

4

No, if there is to be an image for us, for our isolation here and the rigour and intensity of our training, it cannot be that of the monk. It is an outmoded notion that all disciplines which subdue the personal to a larger idea are religious.

The image I prefer is that of the sportsman, living day after day, in every nerve of his body, in every fibre of his will, with an *event*. There is something clean and healthy in that, some vision of open air and horizons that seems more appropriate to us than the pale recluse. And especially those sportsmen who train in groups but will, at the last moment, act alone. The giants of our epoch are those lone figures whose real antagonist is themselves, even when their 'self' takes the form of a glassy peak in the Himalayas or an ocean or a desert or a stretch of time to be endured out in the vastness of space. An early flier like Lindberg, for example, taxies off to cross the planet on a fixed route that can be plotted on a chart, to cover a known distance from one point, named and with a history, to another named point – Roosevelt Field Long Island to

Paris France – but is adventuring, in fact, into the pure space of himself. It is not distance or air currents or a mathematical equation of air-miles against fuel consumption that he is in competition with but his own capacity to endure solitude, to drive a big frame with heavy bones that demands to be horizontal, and blood that lies in pools or trickles through narrow channels, from one point in time to another that is still invisible beyond the furthest horizon.

So, there it is, the ideal. We are swimmers, skiers, long distance runners, test pilots, walkers in space.

I think especially of that marvellous Japanese who set out to ski down Everest, living for all the months of his training with the mountain itself in his imaginary sights; letting his body breathe with it, taking its strange light into him as the sun up there struck cold off snow steeps and jagged ridges, its planetary silence in his skull, its flamelike air ablaze on the surface of his skin, its outcrops and crevasses shockingly concealed under whatever snow-run he was making, even in easy practise on the softest home fields. Then, at the end of long months, the haul to his unusual starting-point – the summit, and the measuring by slow steps, one after the next, hour after hour, in breathlessness and extreme bodily fatigue, of every centimetre of what he will cover later in just a few ecstatic seconds; and behind him as he climbs, set up in reverence at every stopping-place, the little mirrors in which the mountain's spirit is caught and reflected, the great antagonist.

Slowly, day after day, in imagination, I am climbing

towards the *event*. At the moment when it takes place I shall be flying, tumbling, skiing down all the hours of my sitting here day after day, my papers and photographs and newspaper cuttings flashing past now in a continuous stream, too fast to be read, but every fact recognized, known and brought into focus in the high strange air, in the piercing light of it and of the little mirrors I have set up to catch and hold its spirit, the pure, accessible sky peak.

5

Spread out on the desk where I work are half a dozen photographs of the piazza at P., together with a detailed plan of its four cross-streets and the various entries and exits. By putting the plan and the photographs together I have developed a clear notion of the place, but it has gaps, and the gaps worry me.

When laid out in series the photographs make a complete three-hundred-and-sixty degree view.

On the western side of the piazza, the church of Sant' Agostino that gives its name to the square: early fourteenth century, with one unfinished tower. To the north, across a busy cross-street, the public gardens. Arcaded shopfronts to the east, below a nineteenth-century mock-Renaissance façade. Then a second cross-street, without traffic, and closing the square at the southern end, a fortified gothic palace.

The gaps are not in the physical picture that presents itself to me (which I have built up through long hours of fixing my attention on the photographs so that they form a continuity in my head) but arise, as one might predict, from the difference between knowing a place in your five senses, as a three-dimensional space in which you move and breathe (from having actually been there and experienced, for example, the relative difference between your own height and that of an unfinished tower) and a knowledge that has been arrived at by induction, in which every detail, however sharply observed and recorded, has by-passed the senses altogether. The gaps, I mean, are in myself.

The photographs themselves are very striking. They have been taken by one of our agents, a professional in this business. I imagine him posing as a tourist, standing there in the sunlit bowl of the square and making his seven shots, *snap*, *snap*, *snap*, in a perfect circle. It is into the shape of this make-believe tourist that I slip when I enter the square, and through his eyes that I see the place; which means that as far as my knowledge goes, the Piazza Sant' Agostino at P. exists entirely in its own space. Of P., a small provincial town of no particular distinction, I know only a single piazza, sunlit, pigeon-crowded, hanging in mid-air, and surrounded in my vision of it by perpetual fog.

This then is the scene of the crime, a place approached not by ordinary streets where families live and traffic moves, where things are made, bought and sold, consumed, broken, but by weeks of careful preparation. It is not a playground, this piazza, for teen-age footballers, a crossing point to another part of the town, or a gathering place for young and old, but a stage-set awaiting events, and its appearance, after so many centuries, in the light of 'history'.

So then, let me take my imaginary walk around it, beginning with photograph number one.

What I have before me is the unfinished façade of the church, a clear expanse of golden plaster, roughened here and there with brickwork and broken by a rose window with six marble spokes and three ornamented doors.

The effect of roughness is exaggerated in the photograph because the sun is slanting in from the north-west, casting heavy shadows, and the same elongated shadows fall (I almost said flow, since they have the consistency of slow tar or lava) from the steps that lead down into the piazza from a platform that runs the whole length of the façade. There are four steps in all, and the platform, which is five or six metres wide, is of flagged stone. It provides, at this hour, a playing-space for a group of schoolboy footballers. They are wearing sweaters pushed up at the elbow, and their jackets can be seen in a pile on the steps, so I guess it is autumn or early spring, about four-thirty in the after-noon. Judging from the size of the pile there must be thirteen or fourteen of them.

The player closest to the camera is, of course, larger than the rest; his head and one shoulder are blurred. He is moving in fast to where the ball is rising towards him at thigh level. You can see its shadow on the wall.

Six other boys appear in various postures and at various distances from him, and several of them recur in later shots; but some of the players, one guesses, never appear at all, though they were clearly present all the time the square was being photographed. This is because our photographer, following his own needs, was moving in a continuous circle from right to left, while the football game, following the unpredictable flight of a ball and the players' attempts to place themselves in its path, was in violent progress all about him.

So here too is a gap. Several of the footballers, though they too were in the square, simply failed, in the disorderly bunching and shuffling of the game, to get recorded. They exist only in the gaps between shots, like the noise the players were making, their shouts of 'Here!', 'To me!', 'Faster!' which are also absent and represent a deficiency in the photographer's art.

So then, details.

I note the four steps and the width of the platform. Moving close in, using a glass, I note that the central door of the church, a fine bronze with monumental hinges, is permanently closed. A woman in black carrying two plastic bags has just emerged from the door to the south, scattering the shadows of a dozen pigeons across the façade. Another figure, having already descended the steps, is moving off (we see only her back) towards the cross-street. The door of the church is still swinging behind someone who has just entered, or is being pulled back by someone who has yet to emerge. No action, except from the footballers, at the north end of the façade, and the lintel over the north door, and the platform in front of it, are crusted with droppings. Only the south door is in use.

This is the door he will emerge from.

The crime will take place on the platform, or on one of the four steps leading down from it, on the south side of the square.

The second photograph shows just such a place. In this shot the old woman who has just emerged from the church is about to step down into the well of the square, and the woman whose back we saw in the previous photograph is in profile, but too far off to be clear. She is crossing the narrow street towards the gothic palace, her head turned to take account of an approaching cyclist.

The palace I call gothic has one large central gateway leading to a courtyard. No windows, but a loggia with six pointed arches about halfway up, then crenellations and a square tower with a pole. The street that leads away beyond it into the town is dark and narrow (the first of the two women seems to be moving towards it) and reveals nothing, either of itself or of what lies beyond, since it almost immediately makes a deep arc. No amount of peering or moving up close with the glass will take me further along that street, but I continue to stare at it, as if I could somehow, by sheer will-power, set the woman's stopped figure in motion and follow her round the curve.

A safe part of the square, this. Quiet. There is no post for observation (even the loggia is blind), nothing is happening. The end of the street is closed off with three bollards and a chain, so that the cyclist who is approaching (illegally it seems) will have to pass between one of the bollards and the palace wall.

It is the part of the square I feel most secure with. I

have become quite fond in a way of the cyclist (a fat man in a beret) and of the two women who have appeared at just this moment and are, for me, the familiars of this side of the piazza, enlivening its uneven flags with their presence. The one with the two plastic bags stoops with their weight. The other is also stooped, but the weight she carries is invisible. They must have been to vespers, or have slipped into the cool church to pray for a moment or to be alone in that still place with the spirits of the dead, a husband or a son lost in the war. It would please me – I mean I would find it a comfort – if they could be there at the time of the event; I have got used to them. Though in fact their faces are so unclear that I wouldn't recognize them if they did appear, and who knows what their habits are and what they are normally engaged in at this particular hour? (*Is* this the hour? Is that why the photographs have been taken at – I am guessing – between four-thirty and five in the afternoon?)

We move on past the palace to the intersection. Traffic approaches at right-angles here and turns west. There is a paperstand at the corner with a striped awning, then the bollards that close the street. More bollards and chains close the extension of the main street along the western edge of the piazza, and in front of them several motorinos are parked, some with the riders still astride, and more young people are strung out in the sunlight towards the middle of the square.

This is a social corner, you see that immediately. Strange the dynamics of the thing. The activity that begins here extends into the next photograph, which shows part of the arcaded shopping area, with more bikes and more young people milling around what appears to be a café or ice-cream parlour. Yes. Examined with the glass, several of these young people prove to be holding cones. One or two of the faces can be made out, especially that of a blond girl whose hair has come loose; she is laughing, throwing her head back, and trying to take the hair from her eyes while holding the ice-cream at such an angle that it is about to topple from the cone. But mostly the faces are a blur. The arcade behind the columns has canvas blinds. At this hour, and at this time of year, the blinds are rolled halfway up. Peering beneath them, again with the aid of a glass, you can make out shops: a café with two long windows, a shoeshop, and what seems from the sacks outside to be a store that sells grain.

The shop-fronts continue unbroken in the next photograph: another café more or less deserted, a window with curtain materials and cushions and at the corner a bank. But this photograph is utterly deserted and the lack of people affects its mood like a change of weather. Even when you put the photographs together and try to take in the whole western side of the square at a single sweep, the disjunction is unmistakable. It is as if one of the shots had been taken on a different day from the rest.

Everything about this view is depressing – the bank with its drawn curtains, the unfashionable café, the shop with curtain materials that nobody is looking at or wants to buy, the sense one has that the piazza slopes to the south (does it? Could one tell that from the lean of the motorinos or the stance of the girls?) and that its life is naturally drawn off in that direction. (Is it because of some inclination of the land itself, and its influence over the centuries, that only the south door of the church is in use?).

But I am haunted by another quality of this view that has nothing to do with absence of people or the fact that the westering sun sets its buildings in deep shadow, flattening their projections and blurring their hard lines.

Turning away from the event, which will have taken place at the south end of the platform – or if more than one shot is needed, on the steps – it is this view that will confront me as I run, my ears filled with the echo of the shots and the cries of bystanders, to where the car will be waiting at the corner beyond the bank. The mood of this photograph belongs not to the time when it was taken but to the moment immediately after the killing. It lacks people because they have been drawn to the commotion opposite. The square has naturally emptied towards the south, and I alone am running in the other direction.

For all its lack of interesting detail, this is the view that has most to reveal. It tells me what I shall see – and perhaps even how I shall feel – in the moments after the crime. It is a photograph of the future.

The remaining views, showing the north side of the square, seem altogether less important; everything significant, as we have seen, happens at the other end. But it would be intolerable to have a square in your head that was open to the unknown on one whole side.

Photographs six and seven fit neatly together to make a public garden, which from the disposition of the trees, all regularly planted and clipped, must be laid out in formal walks, maybe even with fountains and a pond. A gravel path runs up the centre with an equestrian statue at the point where it is crossed by side paths. The statue is of stone, and the horse has been caught in its progress out of the nineteenth century towards the wide street that runs along the north side of the square, which must, to judge from the traffic, be one of the city's major thoroughfares. (When I reach the car that will be waiting under the arcades of the bank it is along this street that we will make our flight.)

The statue itself remains mysterious. The path on which it stands is almost perfectly bisected where two views join, but when the two photographs are laid side by side a space of one fifth of a centimetre on the scale of the photographs (nearly half a metre in reality) is missing, and the horse's head and the rider above, all but one hand extended in a rhetorical gesture, are in the gap. Another little imperfection in the photographer's art, but one that I find oddly re-assuring, since it is into just such a gap in reality (though rather wider, I hope, than a fifth of a centimetre) that I mean to slip in the moments after the crime. Having stepped out of my life to give the event, for that brief moment, the mind, the will, the trigger-finger it needs to come into existence. I shall step out again, as invisible and anonymous as that rider on the horse or our tourist/photographer, whose presence here we must take as given, since these views could hardly exist without him, but who is nowhere to be found in them and cannot be traced as their source.

So there it is, the Piazza Sant' Agostino at P. Of P. itself I know nothing; and of the square no more than I need to know. It is flagged, with big paving-stones, some of them stamped with the city's crest. It is closed on three sides with buildings, each of different centuries, and open to nature on the fourth. It has existed in this form since the 'nineties, and has been called the Piazza Sant' Agostino since the foundation of the church five centuries ago. Innumerable events have taken place here, some of them historical, some of them no more important than the appearance at the south door of the church of my two old women, who are commemorated in photographs one and two, the seven footballers with their invisible ball, and that crowd of young people whose presence here, and the shifting associations between them as they move from group to group, talking, exchanging gossip, making dates, will lead to other events – marriages, quarrels, bitter separations – too numerous to contemplate.

I have been in this square a hundred times in imagination. I shall enter it only once in fact, and may never know more of it than I do now, since the event itself, and the heart-slamming moments that lead up to it, will leave me no time for looking about to corroborate the thousand details I have stored in my memory. I shall be in the square for less than three minutes if all

37

goes well. If it does not, the time, and the details, won't matter.

Meanwhile the event that will make this place notorious, that will take its name from the piazza and may prove to be the point in history towards which, through all the centuries, it was quietly moving, is still to occur, and only I can precipitate it. This knowledge gives my vision of the place an added dimension. It brings to the flat, black-and-white shots an excited glow as of a place that I have known already in a dream. And for me it will always be like this. Even when the brilliance of these separate visions has been dampened somewhat by real weather, and real sunlight being soaked up and reflected by stone. I have seen the square already in the light of its notoriety. After the event.

Someday in the future – let us say twenty years from now – I may return as a genuine tourist, though with a special interest; perhaps even in the company of a wife and child; stopping off out of whatever ordinary life I shall have slipped back into to revisit it. And in a sense I have already moved past the event to that nostalgic view that is inherent in the photographs, and perhaps in the very nature of photography itself. I am nostalgic for what has not yet occurred: for the darkness my first old lady is crossing towards, where the narrow street on the east side of the palace curves out of view; for the bean soup she will cook, and the headlines her husband will read aloud from the evening paper: ASSASSINATION AT P. This is the one indulgence I allow myself. It is purely aesthetic and therefore harmless.

But I wonder sometimes – to return to those gaps – how far I can trust my senses. I place my fingertips on the rusticated stone of the palace and try to feel the roughness. I try to judge whether the platform steps when I touch them are still sun-warmed or already cold. But imagination goes only so far into the world of touch, and though there is something to go on there is never enough. And how does the piazza smell? Of manure? Of fish? And is the sea audible at times under the hum of the traffic or when it pauses at the lights? I go back and back to the place and know from the triangle of shadow at its corner every uneven stone in the pavement. But I come as a man who is deaf, who cannot feel the warmth of the sun or the sudden cool-ness of shade, who has no sense of smell; a ghost, a tourist/photographer/assassin composed of nothing but mind.

It is to deal with at least one other of the senses that I imagine myself buying an icecream at the corner café.

Today the square tastes of chocolate. Tomorrow will be coffee and walnut, the day after pistaccio. A different flavour for each day of the week.

6

Do I need to name him, our great man of letters? He is a household word. Even those who have never read a line of the elaborate prose, whose authority is all in its fine distinctions, in its capacity to hold several opposing views in the same steady vision, may find one of his simple phrases on their lips in a moment of supreme emotion or will be aware at least that he is, at eighty, a rare national treasure and the last great figure of the age, a surviving witness to its many splendours and the long procession of its woes.

Essayist, philosopher, author of a dozen monuments to the art of narrative, he has created so much of our world that we scarcely know where history ends and his version of it begins. A whole stretch of the century lies exposed in his work: populations driven this way and that from farm to city – the poor, the hopeful, and those who already have no illusions – dark transports bearing them, across a countryside poised tremulously on the point of change, to factories, slave camps, pits of official slaughter, front line ditches at the edge of night. His vision is epic, and it is an epic strength that he brings to its depiction; yet no one has written more delicately, or with greater compassion and tact, of life's ordinary occasions, of first love, first tears, or the taste of that first mouthful of bread a boy pays for with his own earnings; of women seated alone with a suitcase in the waiting rooms of enormous stations, who have nowhere to go because they do not have the price of a ticket; of a child who eats apart in the playground to hide his secret shame – there is nothing in his lunch tin; of a youth so enamoured of his own purity that he cannot accept from the girl who comes to him her pure and common gift; of other, poorer youths brought face to face at last with their own future in the form of an examining committee or an agent of the law – Injustice in all its official regalia; of a workman, bestially drunk, who has been shamed once too often by his wife's forgiveness and beats her mercilessly in the public street. He has a special feeling for these dramas of the defeated. But for all his insistence on human folly and waste, and for all the darkness of his view, he never loses sight of the fact that day by day, even in the years of deepest horror, the life of things continues in the old patterns and according to the oldest and most ordinary rules. Spring arrives in the midst of battle with the same radiance of pear-blossom and hawthorn and little wild-flowers on banks in the wood. Birds sing above the slaughter. There is a harvest to be got in. A field of barley, sighing like the ocean, its long ears heavy with dew, has its own time-span and cannot wait another day to be brought in, whatever the facts

41

of history. Grapes in September, olives in the clear cold days at the turn of the year. Wholeness and balance – that is the key-note. No other writer reminds us so often, or with such profound conviction, how much of our life is to be discovered, and enjoyed and made use of, in the narrow area between ecstasy and despair.

His conception of the task he has been set, and his strict dedication to its fulfilment, has created a body of work that fills a whole shelf above my desk, volume after volume of grace and light. It has also created the rather stiff and forbidding figure he presents in the photographs, the gaze direct, intense, but inward looking, its challenging frankness a kind of mask. He is, like his paragraphs, all of a piece; but a large piece that takes account of the contradictions and holds them in a precarious balance. 'This', he seems to say (he is not without humour) 'is my special trick. I do it well. It has taken me sixty years to achieve just this mixture of recklessness and ease.'

Pathetically fragile as a youth, and with a tendency to stoop, he has developed over the years a ramrod straightness, and suggests, with his clipped moustache and skullcap of cropped hair, the general of an imperial army, but one grander and nobler in its aspirations than any actual army of any nameable power. It is his struggles at the desk, and the keen self-discipline they necessitate, that has endowed his figure with hardness; as if the achievement of a perfect sentence imposed on the muscles the same rigours as a hundred press-ups or a half-hour's workout on the bars.

As a child he suffered from asthma and from all sorts of minor ailments. Today at eighty he has a constitution that would have astonished the youth of sixteen, and might even have embarrassed him with a robustness too common to be the vessel of extraordinary gifts.

Long-faced, tow-headed, he makes no impression at all in the family albums. He seems to be hiding from something. (Prompted by the author himself, we might guess at this distance that he was hiding from his fate.) It is the elder brother, the mother's favourite, son and heir to what there was of a family fortune, who catches the eye: a tall, clear-browed youth, utterly confident of his place in the world and of his own capacities, radiantly aglow with energy, and so impatient for the future that his glance already flashes beyond the restricting frame, his body seems already to have broken its formal pose, not by any movement of the casually settled limbs but in the animal spirit. He is a lion to the author's lamb.

Early pages of the *Memoir* make much of this contrast between the two brothers. They are filled with the freshness and splendour of the older boy's presence.

On a summer holiday on the Adriatic he is involved in a fist-fight with a young Austrian, and though badly beaten, his jacket torn, his cheek grazed and bruised, he walks away in the full retention of his spiritual ascendancy; the younger brother is much impressed by the light of solitary glory that plays about him as he wanders off through the *pineta*, and the incident

43

becomes a model to which he returns over and over again, in more complex situations, of inner triumph in the face of defeat. The leader in all their childhood excursions, the giver of names to the objects of their common world, the recorder of its landmarks and mythologies, the older boy presides over these first years like a tutelary god.

His death, in the last weeks of the war, was not only the occasion of our author's earliest published work but the turning point, it might now appear, of his life. He has himself related how that first story leapt into existence and surprised him with the fact that he was a writer; and it is typical perhaps that the occasion should be, in retrospect, so full at the same time both of joy in the discovery of his own powers and an irremediable anguish.

He was preparing for his exams in the last days of summer, and had gone off to a favourite hiding-place to read, the top of an old oak tree beyond the orchard. It is famous now, he made it so, but was a special place even then in their secret geography of the region – a point of entry via its gnarled roots into the under-world, and upwards via its branches into the angels' realm.

He must have dozed off. Suddenly, starting awake, he became aware by a kind of sixth sense, before he could possibly have observed him, that his brother was there at the oak-tree foot staring quietly upward, afraid perhaps to startle him in that precarious cradle so high up in the boughs, and so quickened by the exertions of a fast sprint across the fields that the younger boy could hear the fetches of his breath. He must, he decided, have come home on an unexpected leave. He was simply standing, his face raised to the big tree's wealth of green, and breathing so deep in himself that the boy wondered if he had come to seek him after all and wasn't here on some business of his own, he was so completely absorbed in contemplation of the great rich canopy of leaves that poured its light upon him. He seemed too far off to be reached. But after hesitating a moment, the younger boy leaned down from his bough and called: 'I'm here. Come on up.'

The young man seemed caught off guard, as if he couldn't for the moment locate the source of the voice. Then he broke into one of his brilliant smiles, sprang into the boughs and began climbing.

But did not arrive. Passing out of sight for a moment in the thickness of the summer growth, he simply disappeared.

'I knew then,' the old man writes at a distance of nearly sixty years, 'that the few brief seconds in which I waited so breathlessly for him to reappear would become years, would become the whole of my lifetime. He was dead, I knew it quite clearly, in my blood, in the throbbing and quickening of my own pulse. Two days later the telegram arrived. But by then the little story, which had sprung fully developed into my head at first sight of him, had been written. He had given it to me complete, in that moment of staring up out of the darkness at the tree's foot. I have told nothing of this till now. It has been, for all these years, the obscure root out of which all my branches grew . . .'

It is a remarkable achievement, that first boyish effort; a vision of war in which his own imagination, and what he had heard at first hand from his brother, miraculously cohere to create out of children's games and boyish fantasies the whole horror of a generation's induction into the realities of war; a piece of local mythology transformed and expanded, a private vision shot through with the glare of history and made all the more significant by the author's youthful capacity to let everything he knows come flooding into the work, as if this might also be the last of it and he had no awareness yet of the sixty years that stretch so grandly before him, in which what he knows will find its full expression and for which something ought, after all, to be conserved. 'First works are like first love. Never again such prodigality – such thoughtless innocence.'

It was his brother's letters from the front that had done all this – not only opened his mind, in the deepest way, to the loss of youth and all its illusions among the abominations of war, but to those feelings of compassion for the ordinary man and his sufferings that have been so essential to his work. 'Through my brother's eyes', he tells us, 'I saw. That was the vision. And having seen could never forget.' The young god's death imposed upon him, all the more, his duty to remember and bear witness. 'Whenever I have been tempted as a writer to the merely brilliant and superficial, it is the shadow of his life, and the lives of so many in that generation, that falls across the page and recalls me to my solemn task. I began as a ghost writer. Perhaps I have remained one.'

Almost from the day of the brother's death (and his discovery of his own talent – since the two can hardly be separated) he ceased to stand at an oblique angle to the world. It is as if he had more air at last and could breathe deep. Suddenly precipitated into the centre of the family and loaded with the older boy's destiny he found the physical dimensions to fit it: he grew six centimetres in a single year, threw off his asthma, saw that first story, in which all his gifts appear in full flower, published and acclaimed, and arrived in a single bound at the threshold of a career.

In the light of all this, his claim to be no more than the older brother's ghost seems disingenuous, a little too good to be true. One senses rather the joy and confidence of being released into life at last, the transformation of old restrictions, old resentments even, into new forms of power. Like everything else about him, the moment of his brother's disappearance remains ambiguous; and one suspects that the elder boy, however attractive he may seem in the photographs, is little more than a literary device for the dramatization of his own leap into life. Genius is sly as well as candid. Was he perhaps the favourite child all along, that sickly heir-apparent – keeping out of the limelight, protecting himself from the need to be heroic, allowing the first born (as he comes close to suggesting on one occasion) to be the sacrificial victim that his generation demanded? Was he from the beginning the chosen one in the eyes of the gods?

Whatever the truth, he survived, and has come to see the shadowiness of his early life as part of a larger plan. The weakness nature gave him at the start was a way of conserving her own gift of strength, a first lesson that everything, even the gods' most abundant favours, must be recognized and grasped for.

Setting the photographs in chronological order, one observes the straightening and firming over the years of all his lines, but most of all the deepening at the bridge of his nose of two vertical creases like inverted commas – the imprint of a lifetime's devotion to irony. It is the development of a single theme. A slight nervousness, not to say slackness, in the too-pretty, rather girlish chin is there from beginning to end, but assumes over the years a new significance; so too does the tendency to dreaminess in the liquid eyes. These signs of weakness, of a secret complicity with the forces of disintegration, of sensuality, of illness even, are never quite subdued to the austerity of the whole; they remain to complicate the picture, and as the face discovers its sterner characteristics, so the chin becomes finer, more nervously attuned to what tempts to indulgence, the eyes grow deeper, more dreamy. It is as if eyes and chin belonged to a different style of life from the strict mouth and the inverted commas above the nose; brought him news of the underworld; belonged to the author of what he likes to call his anti-Works, those dark, unwritten master-pieces that are in an opposing spirit to his own but are their shadowy complement. It is part, all this, of that delicate balance between moral strictness and a disarming openness to the destructiveness of things that is his signature and constitutes his 'special trick'.

What better example than the essay on Julian the Apostate, so bold, so ardent, so extravagantly wilful, in which the prose itself, phrase by phrase, responds to the two sides of his nature, the natural bohemian and pagan sensualist and that grim apostle of rule and order, that worshipper of the stern god? Impossible in these pages to pin the author down, as his nature turns now this way now that, and his thought moves, in its monumental but oddly quick-footed and quick-witted way, among church ceremonies, theological disputes, banquets, assignations, court intrigues – endlessly shifting between fastidious disapproval and an almost breathless realization of the enticements of the flesh. (The commentators fly amusingly in both directions, like messengers scattering from a battlefield to announce simultaneously, and by their own lights accurately, both triumph and defeat.)

It has always been the same. Invited in the 'thirties, when imperial glory was the very stuff of our daily lives, to contribute to the birthday honours of the regime's favourite historian, he first declined, then hesitated, then ruefully accepted, then produced nothing at the right time, then, at the wrong time, not the middle-length essay he had been asked for but a whole brilliant book, a flight of scholarly fancy on the subject of Roman drains that was immediately taken up by the opposition and read, in all its twistings and turnings through the intestinal underworld of the imperial ideal, the darkness under crowded theatres and stadia and forums, as a deliberate attack on the notion of empire itself.

A savage battle raged, from which he remained grandly aloof, expressing nothing but surprise at the way his little researches had been taken: 'Scatology? Do they really think so? Subversive? My humble drains?'

Friends pointed out the danger he was in and urged him to flee. He shrugged and prevaricated; but before the authorities could come to their ponderous decision, took his wife and the three much-photographed children and went, carrying with him all his household effects: library, stamp collection, Persian rugs, cabinet of antique coins and bronzes; but defiantly, under the very nose of the police.

There followed six years of voluntary exile, first in Switzerland, then in Argentina. They proved of course to be the most productive years of all. When he returned he was indisputably The Master, but with his wife dead and the majority of his friends and contemporaries dispersed or done away with – victims of the convulsions of those years – it was a lonely triumph. Cut off from the new generation, a survivor it might seem from the far side of history, he withdrew, and has over the years become more and more inaccessible, more remote in his solitary grandeur; and this too has added to the lofty image he presents and the power of his presence among us as a sacred monster.

There are photographs as well as volumes of richly worked prose to illustrate this. I lay them out on the desk and use a magnifying glass to bring them close.

Item: from his years of research on the imperial drains a casually perfect image from the ruins at Sabratha. The great man, all clipped and smooth in a light grey suit, with a cane over his shoulder and his thin moustache prematurely whitened by the North African sun, leans diagonally across the frame, in parody one might think of a matinee idol from the cinema or a music-hall performer. On his thin lips there is just the flicker of a smile. As at some subterranean jest. 1933.

Item: from the following year something less poised and formal. He appears as *pater familias* under a striped beach umbrella, with his wife, the three children and the various paraphenalia of their summer play – beach buckets and spades, a ball and an inflatable shark or dolphin, it is difficult to tell which, that the little group has laughingly included as the family pet.

These were happy years. They went out a good deal, the famous couple, and were photographed in many fashionable places. His extraordinary energy involved him in literary activities outside his fiction – criticism, controversy. They were the centre of a brilliant group. They gave parties, had other famous people to stay for the weekend, kept three houses, one in the mountains and another on the coast as well as an establishment in Rome that had always, outside the sacred hours of his labour, an open door for unexpected guests. Fate, and history, had not yet intervened to make a recluse of him.

Item: two snapshots from the Swiss period.

In one the writer is caught (if that is the right word) in his garden. He is again suited in grey, with a checkered bow-tie, and is on this occasion holding in his left hand a straw boater that seems almost transparent in the late afternoon light, a discarded halo. He is leaning forward to examine a rose. To examine it, I mean, in the inquisitorial sense; asking it to account for itself, to say precisely what it means or understands by its own being. He looks faintly amused by the rose's discomfort at being faced, and so publicly, with a *personage*; and one whose mere presence in the garden calls everything else into question. 'See what a terror I can be, he seems to be saying. 'even when I am off duty, even when I am in nature. Such are the rigours of the moral life. Such it is to have greatness thrust upon one. Isn't it a tremendous joke? But tell me this, little rose, am I really the great man himself or just a child dressed up in the great man's clothes?'

In the second of these snapshots he does not appear, but one guesses from the amateurishness of the pose – the family strung out in a single line with three jagged peaks behind them – that the camera was in his hand, and that the distorted shadow that falls across it is his.

The wife Elena is looking away in brilliant profile. The children, two girls and a boy – one girl a leggy twelve year-old, the other just out of the plump infant stage, the boy sitting cross-legged and engagingly alert in knickerbockers and cap – are staring straight into the sun, and are touched for the contemporary viewer by what he knows is already moving towards them out of the decades to come.

The boy will be finished at twenty-two in a shooting

accident. For all his sturdiness he has been bequeathed, and in large measure, the fineness of the famous chin, that pointer to a world of decadence that our great man keeps at a distance with stern discipline, allowing it just enough scope to give fantasy, drama and a sense of risks grandly taken, to his prose. The boy, not knowing the rules of that perilous game, and having no 'special trick' of his own, will take the fiction for fact; he will catch from the swamp element in his father's imagination a chronic fever.

The youngest child will enter an asylum on the far side of one of those sparkling alps, not a hundred kilometres as the crow flies, as the black crow flies, from where she is now standing.

Only the elder daughter will find the strength to survive. But it is the strength of a nature unqualified by any touch of lightness. She will thicken into the sour fifty-year-old, her father's keeper, who will be at his side, guiding him towards me with a strong hand, when we come to the event.

The truth is that his special trick depends upon his playing, quite deliberately, with forces that he is by nature immune to and others are not. He flirts with destructive passions – madness, perversion, the flight into illness – to test his own capacity to resist, to call up the correlative and bracing forces that add tension to his work. But the poisonous vapours released do not immediately disperse. They hang about him; they are transferred from his imagination to the imagination of others and assume real forms there that they are pow-erless to resist. Commentators sometimes speak of him as a tragic figure, as a man to whom the gods have granted every favour but one: he has suffered the loss, one after another, of all those who were dearest to him. I wonder. Like all great men he is at heart an egoist, and dangerous. His wife in the Swiss photograph seems already used up. Her staring away out of the frame is like a first step to freedom; she has set her face against something – Argentina? (She will die on the voyage out and be consigned to the waters off Grand Canary.) The thin-legged girl seems already to have been offered up in her mother's place.

There are times when simply to expose oneself to the hypnotic beauties of his style, to enter the labyrinthine sentences with their tortuous flashings and flarings, is to run the risk of a special sort of corruption, the corruption of the moral. I have come to distrust his high-toned achievements at the very moment when I am most deeply moved by them. I have begun to develop a nose, among all that beautiful architecture, all those noble vistas, those pediments and finials, for the smell of drains – a faculty he might recognize and approve and for which he might bestow upon me, from his great height, a little half-smile of sympathetic approval, the pleasure of a Master at the glimmerings of a slow pupil who improves.

But I should confess that if, through long sessions of study, I have begun to understand him a little, to observe, that is, the dangers that are inherent in the very nature of his 'trick', he has also, and so long ago that it quite scares me, both understood and accounted for me.

Imagine the quickening of my pulse, the cold gathering of sweat on my brow, when I first encountered that novella of his, completed in Argentina in 1939, nearly a decade before I was born, in which he describes the assassin of Professor Celario, the ambassador at Santo Domingo. It is as if he had, in some uncanny way, by one of those intuitions that have about them a touch of the demonic and bring a whiff of black magic, of smouldering flesh, to even the freshest of his pages, taken a quick look down the tunnel of his life and seen me, in the merest flash of a second, standing before him with the revolver in my hand. But not me exactly. Rather a foreshadowing of me in the shape of a young man waiting at a tramstop in Zurich, wearing the garments, as he describes it, of an interesting event, and behind the Zurich youth another, glimpsed the previous summer on the Ramblas at Barcelona, in whom he had sensed just that mixture of subdued violence, idealism, recklessness and nostalgia for the impossibly heroic that was floating about in those middle years of the decade and which he would embody in the seminary student Francesco.

The vision can have given him no more than a fleeting glimpse, and I am not Francesco; but he had seen me just the same. Reading his dark analysis, his infernal speculations about the origins of violence in our age, I felt myself first hot, then cold, as if a hand had been laid upon me in the silence and I might be recognized by any passer-by in the street. I felt anger as well. As if all the things I have so painfully discovered and fought for in my life were, after all, quite common and ordinary – predicted, described, made public a decade before my birth.

Is this an example of how he works, this capacity to grasp a whole text by turning up the merest corner of it, this entering so deeply into the form of things that the very process of their being is made available to him through a single detail, and so completely that his energy need only fill their form in space a moment to recreate their whole life and momentum? I imagine the wry tightening of his lips as he perceives that he has already comprehended me and that I can therefore be dismissed. His superiority is insufferable. I feel as if he had publicly humiliated me, even if no one knows it but myself. Is this mere brooding? He has exposed me as a worm; not because his picture of the young assassin is unsympathetic – on the contrary, as so often in his writing he has discovered as many aspects of the anarchist killer in himself as the noble ambassador – but because what he has so amply set down is, he believes, the whole of what I am and only the smallest particle of himself, because in comprehending me he has also written me off.

A good many of my hours here are devoted to a secret turning of the tables on him. I examine the stiff twenty-year-old, staring boldly past the camera with his high white collar and cap, circa 1919, and the borrowed assurance of his dead brother; or the proprietorial young genius, already the darling of the connoisseurs, upright behind the chair where his new bride sits smiling, one hand on his watch-chain, the other resting, very lightly, on her shoulder; or the figure caught 'among contemporaries' on the quayside at Rhodes, disguised now in beard and panama, turning a glass in his hand; and I say to myself, 'I know where you are heading, sir, and you do not. We may add all these facts and images to one another to make a perfect record of your life, and throw in the novels, the essays, the newspaper articles, the letters, your ambassadorial regalia, your medals, your honourary degrees (including the one from Oxford), and all the unhappy history of your family, and what will be missing is a tiny fact that I have in my head and which does not exist as yet in yours. It casts a different light on all this. It subtly changes the portrait of the twenty-year-old genius because it establishes at last what he was peering at so intently across the years and could not make out: the muzzle of a revolver. It is what accounts for those two little creases in the brow that will deepen with the years. It is the third beside you (proprietorial) and your young wife (with her eye already on the sea off Grand Canary) in the wedding photograph. Its shadow falls across the brilliant conversation, changing the weather of that morning at Rhodes and transmuting even the colours of the half-finished drinks. The place and manner of your death – that I have in *my* possession. It doesn't make things even between us, nothing could. But it helps.

Still, I regret that when we do meet at last it will be too late to ask the questions I would like to put to him and which I have come to feel only he can answer. Our conversations remain imaginary; and my imagination is weak. I go back again and again to the hints he has let drop of what he might have to say to me: a few exchanges of the ambassador and his assassin, that are charged with significance and irony but remain inexplicit, since neither knows the part he is to play in the other's life; something to be read between the lines of the 'Letter to a Son'; something again in a note on 'The Present Generation' where he takes as his text, with a playfulness that is not without malice, a passage from Chateaubriand: 'We must speak of a state of soul which, it seems to me, has still to be described: it is that which precedes the development of great passions, when all the young, active, self-willed, yet restricted faculties are exercised only upon themselves, with neither goal nor aim. The more a race advances towards civilization, the more is augmented this condition of the vagueness of the passions. Finally there occurs a sad situation: the great number of examples which one has before one's eyes, the multitude of books which deal with man and his feelings, make the individual clever without having experienced life. He becomes undeceived without having been deceived. Some desires remain, but there are no more illusions. With a full heart one inhabits an empty world, and without having made use of anything, we are dissatisfied with all there is.' Does he realize how the dismissiveness of that may have worked to make some of us – one of us at least – break out of empty dreaming into the world of events?

Of all his various characters, and I am speaking now not only of his writing but of his life as well, it is the son

I feel closest to, dead at twenty-two in a shooting accident which is also, by one of those exchanges of fact and fiction that occur so often in the great man's vicinity, prefigured with uncanny accuracy of detail in one of the *Tales*. But there is nothing more to be discovered in that quarter. The boy makes his brief appearance in family photographs and in clippings here and there from the magazines. He is said to be writing a novel, but it never appears. He does publish poems, but they are not distinguished. He organizes a safari to East Africa and is photographed with lions; he joins a yachting party to the Greek Islands. Then, out of the blue, the accident, and a year later, on the boy's birthday, the 'Letter'.

It is a work that angers me. I resent it, as the son might also have done had he lived to receive it. There is no doubting the old man's grief; he recalls the early years of his own career when the boy was born, adding one or two of those charming touches that are his alone, in which we glimpse something of the young father's pride and affection and something too of the boy's early grace and promise. But there are no letters from the son, no youthful outpouring of reproach or self-justification to which the great letter might be a reply. What the occasion produces is yet another display of stoic fortitude, another act of dedication to the task, and once again – a response we might feel to the demands of the writing itself for 'difficulty' – the insistence on 'taking things hard', on putting himself to the test, on going deep into his nature to track down, at the centre of each labrynthine paragraph, the secret that would hide there and must be dragged into the light and challenged, and disposed of in a cleansing gush of blood. The drama is impressive, so is the passion for truth. But somehow one is embarrassed by the surge of renewed energy that comes to him with this new stroke of fate, the opportunity it offers to show once again his powers of mastery. *The work, the Work.* Everything in the end becomes simply another proof of his extraordinary genius, his capacity to turn life's bitter hardships into the stuff of art.

I say 'simply'; but of course nothing about him is simple. Neither are the reactions he inspires. For the grandeur of the task he has set himself and his patient dedication to its completion I am all admiration. He too is a skier on Everest, and if we find within us the notion of such an ideal, it has been learned from him. (An irony he might savour, this: that he should provide, from the moral point of view, a model for his own killer.) Can genius be separated from egotism? His ego is monstrous; yet it is in the protean transformation and masquerades of this ego, its capacity to slip in and out of other forms, other lives, that he discovers that feeling for the oneness of things that both justifies his vision of himself as a phenomenon of nature and convinces us of its truth. I think of him carrying his precious gift, his ego, before him, like a tribal vessel in which all our destinies are to be read, and have an almost impersonal curiosity about the moment when it will fall from his grasp. It is that sound, its shattering on the stones of the Piazza Sant'

Agostino at P., rather than the shot, his small cry, the daughter's shrill one – it is the thought of that sound, scattering the pigeons across the cathedral façade, filling the square with footsteps, that moves me, and fills me at times with a kind of terror at the enormity of what I am to do.

Tuning my ears carefully as I read – his letters, his stories – I can just hear, faintly between the lines, the first pre-echo of that sound as it lifts and rolls towards me.

7

In cutting myself off from the past and relinquishing every object that might identify me I have made one exception; it is a small one, a variegated pebble I found as a child on the beach at M. and have kept ever since as a talisman. Antaeus retained his strength so long as he could touch the earth, and I suppose we are meant to understand by this fable that there is between us and nature a channel through which energy endlessly flows, and feeds us and keeps us whole. For me, if the analogy doesn't seem pretentious, the earth has contracted to this pebble, once rough-edged, but worn now to a smoothness by years of being turned between thumb and forefinger, as it might, if I had left it out there, have been worn to the same shape by the sea. (I have intervened and changed nothing!)

It is grey, it looks undistinguished. But in certain lights, and when polished by the slight moisture of the fingertips, it reveals hidden colours; muted, but to the practised eye, of a quite brilliant range, like a winter sunset. As a child I used to lie with it so close to my nose that all proportion was lost and I could imagine myself spread out on a clifftop in Sumatra or Peru, watching the tropic sun go down in a vivid light-show on the horizon; or sometimes, in a submarine mood, found myself peering through a thin pane into the mid-ocean depths. Its light could even be perceived with the fingertips, as when, for example, during an examination or in some moment of confrontation in the playground, I turned the pebble in my pocket and felt the occasion instantly transform itself, saw it shot through with new colours, new possibilities, felt myself come to earth as it were, ever so lightly, as if I too had been transformed in proportion with it, on the pebble's smooth translucent surface. Held to the ear like a closed shell I could hear waves in it; not of the sea but from space, a steady beating. Held on the palm of my hand I saw reflected in it the far side of the universe, invisible to us, from which it might have fallen as a fragment of some scattered meteor, still in touch (and I through it) with a million other particles elsewhere, all of them responsive still to the tide of energy from 'out there'.

Schoolboy fancies, all. But they have persisted. Not because I believe them, or have been unable to give up a childish habit of thought, but because they evoke in me real responses that have nothing to do with the fantastic and which still nourish and sustain the spirit.

So: this fragment of my past, this pebble. Always there, a tiny added weight, in my left-hand pocket among the change. I think of it as a source of strength, but it might, I suppose, be my last weakness. A comforter. As a small child I used to let it sleep in my mouth like an all-day sucker, and liked the notion of its being worn smooth there by the words I uttered round it; till my father objected to the impediment in my speech. Now somehow that notion appeals to me again: a stone worn smooth by speech, every syllable, true or false, making its small change in the shape of the thing. Of course I am too old for such nonsense, but I think perhaps, if taken in and questioned, it might comfort me to have the old stone in the corner of my jaw, to taste its no-taste as of space, and to recognize the power of distortion its presence would create and the odd light it might throw on my 'story' – a lurid glow.

I finger it as I write. Does it add its lurid glow even to this?

8

My father comes from a family with land holdings in the south, in Calabria and Sicily. He cut all ties with that feudal world more than thirty years ago, when he was still a student, invested what money he had in a farm, and has lived ever since the life of a gentleman peasant, managing all the farmwork himself and spending his spare time reading, playing the flute, indulging a taste for obscure scientific speculations and mounting one of the country's largest collection of beetles. He is an old-fashioned radical, and believes, I think, that our great mistake was to have left the eighteenth century. He has settled there very happily himself, with just the sort of uncomfortable rigour that would, he affirms, be the salvation of us all. Though fiercely anti-clerical he is not at all irreligious. To watch him surveying, in the early light of a summer morning, a field of wheat that is ready to be harvested, all afire in the dewy moments after sunrise, is to see a man solemnly absorbed in the oldest form of worship. With all this he has a high regard for machinery and is a subscriber to the best journals of contemporary science. He is, I think, almost entirely admirable and a little foolish. In which he once again remains faithful to his chosen century.

For example, nothing that lives, not even a viper, may be killed on his land. When the local electrical authority claimed the right to run power-lines through a section of his woods, he first fought them in the courts, and then, when he had been defeated at last, made them paint the poles. They stand out all the more clearly now, a liverish green, against the changing colour of the hills, and his point is established, but against the grain, not with it. Having first denied the twentieth century, and being forced at last to see it come marching across his property, he has the satisfaction at least of having exposed its vulgarity. His real master is Quantz, whose flute sonatas and studies fill his evening hours; in despite he would want to claim of their original performer, whom he thinks of as a false hero of the age and whose presence, perhaps, his devotion to the flute is intended to exorcise; he is re-writing history. I hope I describe him with all the ironical affection I feel for this old man who is my father, and make it clear that there is nothing in what I have chosen to do that is in any way meant to defy or shock him. It is not my father I have set out to kill. That sort of psychological short-hand is just what he most despises in our century, and in that way I am his true son.

I write to him regularly and look forward to his long, carefully composed replies, with their news of confirmations in the world of astronomy or astrophysics of his own intuitions. One might believe that giant telescopes in the Arizona desert or in Siberia are nightly tilted at the heavens on his behalf, to prove a contention that has long made him seem harmlessly crazy to his friends, and that quasars, and all sorts of other phenomena, spring into existence only so that he can say, 'There, I told you so! Your father isn't such an old fool after all', or to win an argument taken up twenty years ago with one of his eighteenth-century antagonists, or with my mother, who was religious in the conventional sense and regarded all those scientific interests of his that couldn't be pinned to a board and named, and numbered, as little better than witchcraft. A good deal of his talk to me, I have often suspected, is really directed at my mother, whom I barely knew. I do not resent this either. It makes me feel closer to both of them. What I know best of my mother is what he recognizes in me that he can speak to.

It disturbs me that in this period of isolation I am forbidden to write to him. Several weeks ago I manufactured half a dozen postcards, affectionate jottings that are to be posted to him from London at intervals of a week or so till I am released. I have a clear image of him tramping down to the postbox to collect these cards, carrying them up to the house, finding his spectacles and deciphering the brief, false messages. What worries me especially, I think, is the tampering with time. Choosing to write to him from a point three weeks ahead, a postcard from the future, I might equally have postdated the card February 1998, or backdated it to the day Leibnitz died. The ambiguities of shape and direction that are inherent in our idea of time he will argue about by the hour; but he would be affronted, I think, to find me playing ducks and drakes with it in this trivial and easy way. Quite apart from what he might feel about the deception as it touches him, I am treading here on holy ground and being as blasphemous as if I had despatched a series of directives to him in the name of the Holy Ghost.

I saw him last five months ago. He likes me, when I can, to come and spend a few days in the only place I have ever thought of as home; to restore my links with the house itself, but also, since it is in the familiar objects and order of the house that he has settled our relationship, things that are clear and tangible, with himself as well. The familiar warmth of the stone kitchen on early winter mornings, as we sit together at the wooden table drinking coffee from chipped bowls while half a dozen dogs stretch on the flags and new-born puppies moil about in a basket beside the range, or the deep shadows the farmhouse beams make in the light thrown upward by lamps – these are not simply qualities of the place but stages in the day's progress, that have, over long years, become the visible conditions of our common life, all the more deeply felt because they seem independent of us and have only to be stepped back into to be renewed. A house may establish a state of feeling as well as a design for living.

He is a believer in deep continuities, my father, in the shaping influence of scenes and objects on the inner life; these, and the seasonal routines of the farm. To draw me back into them occasionally, into the rituals of my earliest childhood, is he feels to re-enforce for me the clear line of my movement through space and time, even if it has been a movement away.

I am not so sure. But the place itself, and the slow pace of our lives there, in which even our walking is determined by the slope of a field or the roughness of a path on which rain has exposed all the original rocks, the dependence of our diet on the capacity of the land itself to produce in its various seasons this crop, that vegetable – broadbeans, runnerbeans, artichokes, tomatoes, zucchini – imposes its own pattern, and releases us, since it is the pattern of an earlier exis-tence, from what is merely 'modern'. Or seems to. Moving together in it to repair a roughstone wall, or sweating to clear some patch of the orchard that has gone too quickly to blackberry scrub, going through the motions of one of the immemorial tasks of this coun-tryside, as on ladders set at different angles we work fast at the stripping of an olive, the same fruit on the same branch, discovering again, in the rhythms of the work, a silent community – all this is restorative of the old relationship between us, and in my case at least (for he does not change) of an earlier self that I fall back into as soon as my body adapts to the routine of swift, mindless work. The mind lapses, afloat in a slow dream of doing just this and nothing else through all eternity, of working high up in the light of ancient branches, tumbling the fruit into a basket, or when the hand misses, letting it fall into a net. That earlier self is not lost in me, though I reject it. It is for his sake, but perhaps also for my own, that I come back two or three times a year and let it emerge.

Last November, when I was preparing myself for my life here and had in spirit already entered it, I went to visit him for what I knew might be the last time. My lack of absolute presence cannot have escaped him, though he would never have mentioned it.

It was, I know, his favourite time of year, as it is also mine. The countryside is at its barest, showing clearly again its original lines, the fruit trees already stripped, and the woods, in the hollows between fields or on the mountains behind, all the darker and greener for having the scene to themselves at last. The fields, newly ploughed, show all the earth colours, from silver-grey and blond through brown of every shade to the richest loamy black, looking oddly, where plough-lines take shadow in the evening light, as if lengths of woven fabric had been spread to air, knitwear or tweed, and above them the high rinsed skies, with tons of water swirlingly suspended above the blue.

Everything is at a point of rest. The land is waiting to be sown and for the first rain. Stove-lengths of holm-oak, mulberry, acacia have been brought in and stacked in rectangles at the edge of a path. The olive picking is done. There are long stretches of time to be filled with flute-playing in the early afternoon and with small tasks like the mending of tools, the preparing of canes for next year's staking. It is a time of talk; of standing at boundary fences and listening regretfully to the *pock pock* of rifles as hunters drop pheasants on the far side of a hill or the confused medley of sound, horses, dogs, the shouts of men and the reverberation of big double-barrelled shot-guns, at a boar hunt.

Something of the tension between these two aspects of the scene, the land's intense stillness and suspension and the eruption of the sounds of hunting, of men gratuitously imposing their will on things, is what attracts me to this time of year: argument and counter argument, dreamlike stasis and abrupt, violent activity. It would not be the same without its small, unnecessary deaths.

It is a tension that I associate with adolescence, when I first began to think for myself and found, not without pain, that some of what my father most deeply believed and had taught me I could no longer accept. I bought a shotgun, which I kept at a neighbour's house, and I too, when the season came, stalked the wet fields and took my toll of the birds. It was a first disloyalty. My father never found out; or if he did he kept me from my own shame and gave no sign of it. Something of the static quality of the autumn landscape, that sense I had then of being held back from action but criminally freed, still haunts me. It is the landscape of my youth. Though in fact it is my father, these days, who plays the adolescent – the shy, secretive one, full of dreamy yearnings and fulfilments that he cannot reveal.

For the past three years he has had a woman, a village girl not much older than myself, who cooks, cleans the house, looks after a herb garden and chicken-run beyond the kitchen, makes jam, fills the window sills with pots of red and pink geranium and is altogether good-humoured, thoughtful, efficient and clearly fond of him. The house is filled with her companionable warmth, and the occasional flash beyond a door of her pretty headscarfs, and it isn't only the glow of polish and elbow grease that she imposes on all its scattered bits and pieces. I hear her singing sometimes, but the moment she catches my footfall she stops, as if even that might be a presumption I would resent. She serves us in the dining-room at lunch and dinner, quietly fetching and carrying and then eating alone afterwards in the kitchen; but when I am not here they must eat together, either by the kitchen fire or on the terrace, and when I caught them once in the tail-end of an argument, it was, I knew, over her refusal to drop this pretence and share the table with us. But that would have been a declaration that might have involved every piece of furniture in the room.

It was a declaration he wanted to make and which I would have welcomed, but some delicacy of feeling, either on my behalf or the woman's, prevented him. It would have made things easier between us and would have allowed me to move about the house without fear of stumbling on something awkward. As it was I had to pretend that I didn't notice the flow of energy between them whenever she entered a room or when she moved about the table as we ate, the attraction of his attention away from whatever we were discussing, his quickened, almost boyish excitement. More than anything else it made me feel old; as if we had switched generations. In my self-conscious adolescence it would never have entered my head to sleep with one of the girls who came to cook or clean for us; though he must, I suppose, have expected it and kept his eye open for a betraying gesture; as I tried now to keep mine closed.

I had wanted before I left to say something to him or at least to give him a hint that I understood and approved. Especially on the last night, when after our silent meal we had to go out and search the thicket for a strayed sheep.

It was a still cold night full of stars. Thin mist lay in the wooded pockets, but the fields above were silver in the moonlight and as we strolled back we heard the woman's voice from the house; it must have been magnified by the stillness of the night. She was washing dishes at the sink and singing. He stopped to catch the sound, just as we passed the point where it became audible, and I felt him, after that, being drawn on its long, sure thread. A full-throated singing in the old style – a tune that might have gone back centuries, solemn but not sad, and for him an essential quality of the night itself, so that when we paused at the gate to light our cigarettes and he said, not at all embarrassed, 'It's so beautiful; I feel sometimes that I might live for ever,' he was speaking equally of both, the strong hold of the woman's voice and the moonlit land under its ceiling of winter cloud.

'Do you think at all of getting married?' he asked me suddenly.

73

I saw that what he was really telling me was that he would like a grandchild, that that sort of continuity was also in his mind. The woman's voice drew him to the house, but for my sake, and for this, he would delay his going.

'Perhaps,' I said. 'Yes, certainly. In time.'

'Good. It's a fine thing, marriage. I wouldn't want you to miss it.'

He rested his hand very lightly on my arm, then moved off. 'When you were away in America' he said, 'I thought you might never come back.'

I shook my head in the dark, and it was then that I might have spoken, warned him in some way that I had work to do that might take me further from him than I had ever been before, though that too would make no break between us. But it was too late. We were already in the clear light that leapt from the house. The girl had seen us and stopped singing. We were at the boundaries of that early morning silence in which we would breakfast together, finding words only for the yelping and nuzzling dogs, and part on the local platform with only the briefest and most formal embrace, an assurance that everything between us was as it had been and would be always, but with nothing said on either side of what was closest to our hearts.

9

I know every detail of his daily routine. He is, after all, a worker like ourselves, tied, as he has been for more than fifty years, and wherever he might find himself, to a regimen that has, in all that time, barely varied. He is both Master and slave.

Wakes at a quarter past seven to the thin piping of swallows glimpsed in the oblong of the half-open window, their reflection cutting so vividly across its watery light that they seem at moments, by some special trick of their own, to have slipped through into another dimension, since they are nowhere in the room.

Little bodies made of water and dust, the realest thing about them their cries, they are wheeling and dipping in the great well of air below the sill, following the flight of insects, swerving so close to the wall in their frenzied hunger that the shutter, and sometimes even the window-glass, is splashed with their droppings – a nuisance to the girl who has to come and scrape it off, but to him, as he tells us in the *Memoir*, a kind of comic blessing. Especially when a small pile lands splat on his desk; or even – O sacrilege! – on one of his sacred pages, and dries to a crust, and so finds its way into an American library.

The room at S., seven kilometres from P., is a big front room in the second story with French windows to a balcony. There is a view, to judge from the pictures, across low hills, a patchwork of olive groves and vineyards, and on clear days a flash of the sea.

It is the country of his childhood and the house is the one he was born in. He has come, as he says, full circle: one life, a single gesture, the breath and the work.

The room and its contents he has already described in the first chapter of the *Memoir*. I paraphrase.

Walls white – though they were, in his mother's day, pale blue, and there are tiny patches of blue still visible (he has tracked them down, every one, these remnants of the blue skies of his youth) in odd places round the skirting boards and high up in corners under the beams. 'Thankful I am, on occasion,' he tells us, 'for the slapdash workmen of this region, who have left me these scraps of earlier days, the blue of my childhood and youth, to launch back into on invisible parachutes. *Ecco!* We are back in the first days of the century, in mama's room, taking a sip of her early morning chocolate . . .

The walls, now, white, and the curtains also white; an austerity broken only by two eighteenth-century landscapes in rococo frames, and on the sofa-table a fine pre-Columbian terracotta of the earth mother, half human, half animal, squatting in the act of birth.

A bed of the high old-fashioned sort, with brass rails

and finials and a cover in hand-worked crochet. To the right a walnut commode that once housed a chamber-pot, now his night table, and on the marble top an oil-lamp converted to electricity, with a beautifully moulded hood in mother-of-pearl glass. When it is lighted, softly aglow above the fields, it is as if a jellyfish, one of the great medusas, had wandered in from the sea and were pulsing and pulsing, making its way through the depths towards dawn. Besides the lamp, his moderate requirements for the night: pills, a pad and pencil, a tumbler of water covered with a lace cloth.

There are two comfortable chairs in the room, one of them set permanently with its back to the window; it is where he reads in the afternoon. A cabinet for papers, a sofa-table, the big desk – nothing more. Rugs in the winter, the worn stone floor in summer. To the left his bathroom and dressing room, to the right the corridor.

Six days a week he lives and works here, going down only to stroll for an hour before tea on the lawn above the garden and to dinner at eight-thirty. No more visits to the theatre, no public engagements, no trips.

Everything timed precisely.

At seven-fifteen the daughter appears with coffee and an English water biscuit. She kisses his brow, sets down the wooden tray with its worn picture from the Villa of Mysteries at Pompeii, puts his slippers in place on the rug, goes into the room next-door to run his bath-water and lay out his clothes. At seven-thirty he bathes and dresses. At eight-thirty – at the very moment when I am settling at my own desk in the office, to go through my photographs and clippings – he lays out papers, unscrews his pen and begins. He likes to work these days in the room where he sleeps, with the bed in which he takes his night-journeys neatly made behind him, a counterweight to the heavy desk, and the script that rises to fill the blank pages continuous now with his dreams. The swallows are still screaming in circles below. The sound of a tractor can be heard from a nearby field, and from the yard the voices of women. A ground-bass: reality. The words appear.

He writes steadily till just before twelve, when the dog Manfred, a german shepherd, is let in to be wrestled with a little and to lick his hands.

The dog, of course, is famous – either this dog or one of its forebears. A whole essay has been devoted to him, another proof that for the writer material is always to hand, and more of it than he can ever deal with; all there in the room, or in his head. The dog, the domesticated wolf, is the starting point for a disquisition on the long relationship between man and the animal kingdom of which man is himself a part, on the creative energy, the moral energy even, that belongs to our animal nature, its essential innocence, and on our need to make contact with it again, to find our way back into the garden and lie down, in all our dangerous knowledge and power, with the beasts.

The dog is led out again when his daughter appears with his lunch, and she also takes with her whatever he has spent the morning composing. Further paragraphs of an article, or passages to be worked into the *Memoir*, which will be given its final shape only when he has come to the end of these desultory excursions from which, with all the joy of a child stumbling down from the attic, he brings back brilliant fragments of his life that have not yet found expression in some other form, bits of surviving blue, as he puts it, that the careless workman overlooked and which have the virtue now of being living relics from another age. Or there will be two or three pages of a new novel, parts of which appear regularly in the magazines.

This 'Work in Progress' has a special poignancy. It is, strangely enough, the most youthful thing he has ever done – some commentators might say the only youthful thing he has done. Lighter in touch, more daring than anything he would have attempted in his great days or even ten years ago, it is a kind of scherzo in which his deepest themes reappear in travesty, as if, behind all their grandeur, their imperious graspings after the ideal, their noble solemnities, we were invited to see a group of children dressed up in their parents' clothes, the attic finery of a vanished era. *Child's play*, he calls it; something he had to go back to the house of his childhood and his own beginnings to discover, little lively skeletons who have got out of the closet and are making a jolly row (it is his own expression) on the stairs.

Below, in a room at the back of the house, his morning pages will be typed by a young woman, a student, who comes in for two hours each afternoon and is paid by the page.

She is closely supervised by the daughter, who gave up this task only two years ago and finds a good deal to complain about in the cleanness of the girl's copies; though their aesthetic quality is in fact irrelevant, since the old man will cover them with a dense network of revisions in his small, rather crooked hand. It is on these typed pages, he tells us, that the real work is done. 'Second thoughts, always second thoughts, qualifications, digressions, inspired elaborations. The ground work, yes; that comes straight up from the dark like a strong stem, single and full of sap. The second thoughts, unfolding brilliantly out of the first, are the full tree's lovely greenness.'

When he has finished lunch, rested for an hour and read for another hour with his back to the light from the window, the typed pages are brought up to him, together with a coffee, and he will sit at his desk and let his second thoughts into the room. Then at four-thirty he takes his stick, calls for the dog and goes down to take a walk. The day's work is finished and ready to be typed up.

It is all very methodical. Working thus over the years, keeping steadily to the routine, one creates books enough to fill whole shelves in a library and to keep scores of students at work on bibliographies, variant texts, critical studies of patterns and variations; not to speak of the letters, whole crates of them. He still writes four or five each day, in the late afternoon between five-thirty and seven, keeping carbons of the originals that his daughter will file, according to date and recipient, in the cabinet downstairs.

His day now is almost over. Dinner at eight-thirty; alone with the daughter (who has the household's little happenings to relate – any one of which might be something to build on – material, news!) unless they are to be joined by one of his rare visitors, a foreign publisher or translator or some young writer, often American, whose work has attracted him; or, to the consternation of these more serious guests, some odd character whose experience he needs for his work. Not long ago it was a trapeze artist, and earlier a well-known racing driver who was actually photographed with the old man on the terrace, a unique privilege in these later years.

At eleven, whatever the company, bed: the pills on the night table, the glass of water with its lace covering, the pad and pencil, the dark of his mother's bedroom where as a child he had so longed to come and sleep, believing his sleep here, and his dreams, would be different from anything he had experienced in the nursery above. Then darkness, the depths. In which everything is rearranged, reconciled, flickeringly re-asserted, seen again in a new light and in a dimension free of the restrictions of time; and where none, not even the dead, are ghosts.

Some of it perhaps will be brought up into the circle of the hooded lamp: odd messages scribbled without his spectacles on the night pad, in a room whose walls surprise him with their whiteness. He will come to the surface, thus, twice or even three times in a single night, to leave these jottings for his daytime self to decipher. But in the early hours he goes deeper,

deeper. No messages from there. Till the first swallows call him up with their distant piping and the light of their tiny bodies dipping through and through the room.

Seven-fifteen, precisely. Like clockwork.

Swallows in their pane of liquid sky and his daughter's discreet tapping at the door.

From the hands of beneficient nature, his taskmaster and nurse, another day.

10

I am standing before the mirror in the office entrance wearing a yellow silk shirt, white trousers *à la* John Travolta and a spotted cravat, which I am just tucking in under the floppy collar.

'You look fine,' Carla says, entering the mirror behind me. 'All you need is – here, lift your chin a little and keep your eyes closed.'

'What are you doing?'

'You'll see.'

She is patting my cheek with her fingertips. I open one eye: her mouth makes a line of concentration, but she is grinning, the grin is in her eyes.

We are about to set off for The Dancing. We have been twice before, on each occasion to one of the gay discos in the centre, which are less likely to attract a purely local clientele; where visitors from out of town turn up, and straight groups who have heard that the gay places are smarter, bigger, better appointed and more uninhibited than the rest. We go separately and do not speak, but understand that we are there as a group. We all have special clothes for these occasions.

'There, you can look now.'

I look. She has heightened the colour of my cheek-bones with a touch of make-up and put a dot of it at the corner of my eyes. Somehow it changes the whole shape of my face, emphasizes the darkness of the moustache and sideburns, makes me, I decide, look more aggressively masculine, in the ambiguous style of masculinity that actors project and the models in fashion magazines. Instead of protesting as I might have done a month ago I find myself grinning.

I am supposed to be dour and humourless, and in some ways I am. I am also it seems (or so Carla has disclosed) one of those who will appear at a disco wearing make-up.

I look at myself in this odd fancy-dress and feel extraordinarily liberated. The picture I present, which seems so right for my physical type and generation, is so utterly unlike my real self.

Under cover of my disco clothes I have even dis-covered a talent for dancing.

'You must be a professional,' a girl tells me, who has been following my steps in a way that suggests that we are, for the moment, partners – but only loosely, and only in passing.

The floor-space of the disco is divided into several dancing areas, some on one level, some on another, with open screenwork between. The varied play of red, blue and green lights over the darkness, together with the regular beat of the music, the constant movement of limbs and the shifting partnerships that are created as single dancers move in and out of the crowd, all this induces a sense of disorientation, as if everything – lights, music, faces, the endless parade of oddly-dressed figures – were part of a private hallucination. It is another sort of cover.

You dance with eyes half-closed from one level to the other, passing from red, through blue, to green; alone, glass in hand, on the lookout, on the move – and this is normal. Or you lean against a column in the broken light of a lattice screen while the colours wash over you, and that too is normal. Using your arms, your hips, you shift in and out of the crowd, allowing the steps themselves to determine which of these strangers will fall for a moment into partnership with you: a boy in a spangled shirt knotted above his navel, another dressed as a sailor – or maybe he is a real sailor – two look-alike cowboys, a girl in leather skirt and boots, another (or is it a boy?) in some sort of forties costume, flared calf-length skirt in watered taffeta, platform sandals, lids thick with mascara under the piled-up hair. The band thumps too loud for conversation. Words are mouthed in the half-dark. People nod and smile or shrug their shoulders as they do a quick turn and swirl away, already involved elsewhere. When the strobe lights play, figures disintegrate under your gaze, all their movements broken up into disjointed fragments with spaces of dark between that your head fits together to make a continuous sequence.

'*I'm* a professional – an actress I mean. I act with the Baccio di Serpente. Have you seen us?'

It is the girl wearing the forties outfit. She *is* a girl,

and tiny, unusually plain, with a bright ugly mouth and a short chin, but when she says again 'I'm an actress' and poses with her right hand open fanwise behind her head, the chin tilted and the face elegantly frozen, I see immediately what she is aiming at; she is beautiful. She gives an ugly grin and goes back to her dislocated shuffling.

'You must come and see us, we're brilliant. Experimental! Audiences hate us. Once we gave a performance for nine hours in an old warehouse, on a stage made of blocks of ice. We just kept saying the same four sentences over and over in different combinations till the ice was melted. Some Fascists threw stones at us, it was sensational. I'm in a new play now where I come on naked and set a table with everything white: white cloth, white napkins, white plastic knives and forks, but very slowly; it takes half an hour. Then I pour out a glass of milk. Then I take everything off again, very slowly, and drink the milk. Then I come on and do it all over again, but this time everything is black, including the milk. I'm brilliant.'

She dances away in her iridescent dress like a vision out of the past, out of the forties, her eyebrows tragically lifted, blowing kisses.

11

The reality of the crime: a condition that is not at all easy to define.

For me it is already real. I have been living the reality of it for the past six weeks. It is the centre round which my day's every act and thought is rigorously organized. Living as I do now I have nothing but the crime to reach out for and touch. It is my only link with the world.

It is to give the crime form and detail, to make it inevitable in the life of the victim, if not in my own, that I spend so many hours poring over all he has ever said and done, over photographs, newspaper cuttings, scholarly articles, and all the rich outpourings of his imagination, to discover, in that dense tapestry of experience and event, the single thread that leads to the Piazza Sant' Agostino and the muzzle of a gun.

The event must have a reality that demands my presence. Not only at the moment of its occurrence but in these long weeks that lead up to it. The crime must have a logic of which that moment in the piazza is the inevitable outcome.

Of course I know that the reality of the crime has a different meaning for the victim. To be alive is one thing, to be dead another. For him the killing has no reality if he is still shuffling about in his worn slippers between desk and bed, sipping coffee, stroking the dog, getting up out of his afternoon nap to make a tiny correction in what he has written – the correction itself a proof of his continuing defiance of that other reality: *Not this word but that other. There, I have added a comma* – pushing forward another page into the 'Work in Progress', the unfinished masterpiece (yes, it will be unfinished) that I too am obsessed by and whose hero I think of as a mirror image of myself, since every move he makes into the fullness of his existence is a move that holds me off.

The 'Work is Progress' is yet another reality. I have begun to search the career of its interesting hero for clues to my own. Does the Master know this? Has he guessed that he is, in a sense, communicating with me? The idea is less fanciful than it appears. Each word he writes now is a word written in defiance of the end, an end he knows may be as close as his next breath. Is it so fantastic that seating himself each morning at the rosewood desk, at precisely the hour that I begin, four hundred kilometres away, to lay out the materials of my research, bringing to the moment all his powers of mind, will, imagination – is it so fantastic that it should be my presence that moves in to fill the nameless, faceless presence, and that the figure he is creating to keep me at a distance should wear my features? He is a magician, and always has been; dealing as much in the purely imaginary as in the world of facts, his mind strangely open at these moments to the flux of things. It is my entry into his time-flow that is being magically excluded by the 'Work in Progress' and by the imposition between us of his hero.

He fascinates me, this hero, this mirror figure whose every step to the right is a step I take to the left, this angel of anti-death. He has no notion as yet of what the end will be. He goes forward, full of boyish charm and vigour and assurance, five hundred words a day, into the open adventure, towards what I know, and the old man must at least accept as a possibility, is the silence at the end of a page. He has no future, this formula-one racing driver and ex-mercenary who in the last episode was preparing, with a touch of colour on his cheeks and a spot of it at the corner of his eyes, to become the mistress – yes, the mistress! – of a Venezuelan oil-magnate.

For it isn't simply death that the 'Work in Progress' defies with its hero's infinite disguises and transformations, his impudent refusal to stay within the bounds of 'character'; it is the author's whole life's work and the pious expectations of his admirers, the notion that he is already dead and done with, a great figure certainly, but one who belongs to the past. Without for a moment losing contact with himself he has turned his own world inside out, remade himself in a form entirely unexpected and unpredictable. He has discovered within him a being who belongs not to old age but to childhood, and not to the end of life but to the fresh, cruel, innocent, destructive beginnings.

Once again I am lost in admiration. How does he do it? How does he manage decade after decade to find this spring in himself that is in touch with the flow, the change, the renewed life of things? Reading through the works one watches him acquire and cast off a dozen different personalities, the jargon of a dozen careers and crafts (all promptly forgotten, he tells us, the moment he has exhausted their use), the modes of a dozen different forms of the 'contemporary'. Is it true, as he has sometimes affirmed, that there are beings among us so finely attuned to the oneness of things that so long as they go with their own nature they are also going with nature herself, are ceaselessly fed, replenished, renewed by her, and cannot take a false step or fail, cannot die even till the natural force of which they are the vehicle chooses some other form for their energy and grants them release?

Knowing what I do of the end I find this idea disturbing. All I have uncovered of the pattern of his life makes me believe, in his case, in the absolute truth of the theory, if only as he makes it true by the ruthlessness of his own will. What then of me? Am I to step in and break the pattern, to act, as it were, against 'nature'? Or am I too part of the natural order of his life?

It is for answers to this question, some clue, perhaps unknown to him, that is hidden in the twists and turns of a fiction that has the savage and beautiful intensity, the impersonal truthfulness, of a child at play, that I read and re-read the 'Work in Progress'. It is, for all its lightness of touch, an extended conversation with

Death. Who can it be addressed to but me?

Realities:

The crime will achieve its final reality at a point long past the moment of its occurrence either in his life or mine; at the point, I mean, when it is reported. The true location of its happening in the real world is not the Piazza Sant' Agostino at P. but the mind of some million readers, and its true form not flesh, blood, bullets, but words: *assassination, brutal murder, infamous crime, mindless violence, anarchy*. Its needing a famous victim and a perpetrator are merely the necessary conditions for its achieving headlines and attracting the words: we are instruments for the transmitting of a message whose final content we do not effect. The crime becomes real because it is reported, because it is called an *act of terrorism*, an *assassination*, because it threatens *mindless violence* and *anarchy*, because it breaks into the mind of the reader as a set of explosive syllables. These are language murders we are committing. What more appropriate victim, then, than our great man of letters? And what more ironical, or more in his line of deadly playfulness, than this subjection of his being to the most vulgar and exploitive terms, this entry into the heart of that reality (that un-reality) that is the war of words.

I am the perpetrator of the infamous crime in the Piazza Sant' Agostino. That it has not yet occurred is neither here nor there. When it does occur it will have no reality till it has been called infamous and the Piazza Sant' Agostino has entered that litany of place names that need no further definition, being each one as clear a term in the continuing argument, the message received and understood, as *terrorist, brutal murder, infamous crime, mindless violence, anarchy*.

Meanwhile I have begun to see my preparation in another light. In entering so completely into his world, in training myself to respond, minute by minute, to the subtle shifts of feeling and sudden bold intuitions that created it, I am fitting myself to become at last one of his characters, the one whose role it is to bring all that fictive creation down about his ears and to present him with his end.

None of this is actually demanded of me. I am called upon only to be his killer. An act of plain butchery, committed by an impersonal representative of the opposing forces, a people's executioner, would meet all the requirements in the strictly historical sense. But I am no longer thinking of history. This is something done for myself; but also, I would like to believe, for him. So that the moment may have some significance beyond what the newspapers will report as meaningless and brutal fact.

12

Walking home last night I realised that the painters on my corner palazzo, my 'clock', have come to the end of this particular job. The open courtyard was full of their pots, brushes, ladders, planks, and I could hear, from one of the upper rooms where the last of them must have been working, the sounds of celebration. I stopped for a moment to listen. Good sounds, those: bits and pieces of singing, sometimes a lone voice, sometimes two or more; laughter; the explosion of a brief friendly scuffle. Later they came down in their dirty overalls, packed the pots, brushes, ladders on to the back of a truck and drove noisily away. Today other workmen, in blue overalls, are dismantling the scaffolding, and as they do so they call across to one another, tease, joke and pause on occasion to follow the progress along the pavement of a pretty girl.

I am sad to have this fragment of bright activity removed from the scene, but it pleases me to think of the decorators, the same team, unloading their equipment this morning and beginning elsewhere. Soon I suppose the removal men will arrive and there will be furniture to watch being hauled up the side of the building or carried, with curses, up the narrow stairs. New children on the street. New early morning shoppers.

Work. I think of my own work suspended all these weeks and waiting to be taken up again when I am freed. It is that that will define me, work among others – the project shared, completed and the new thing taken up. It is beautiful, it carries one on over all the gaps. It is what I most passionately regretted last night when I watched those workmen come stumbling down the stairs together and heard them tease the youngest, the apprentice, with being drunk and incapable as they loaded up, and heard an older man, when he protested, soothe him and say, 'Come on, lad, 'they're only joking. You're alright'.

This is a time outside my life. Like the others I have lent myself to an occasion, a crime, but will be redeemed immediately after. I shall step into this killing and then step out again. On the other side life, and my real life's work.

13

It has happened at last. The group has been disrupted. One of us has been called.

For some reason I had always assumed that I would be the first to go, that I would step away from a group that was still, till I left it, whole and would support me to the last with its wholeness. Not at all.

This morning we took longer than usual to settle ourselves at our desks. We all have our own little habits for getting down to work, as we have habits for preparing ourselves for sleep. Carla takes a great deal of trouble with her chair. She sets and re-sets it, then begins on her lamp. Arturo stacks and re-stacks the new documents he is to deal with till all the edges are even, then places them squarely in the centre of a desk that has been cleared absolutely of every other object. Enzo likes to sit on the desk, with one foot up on his stool, examining his documents a page at a time, lifting only a single corner; then he turns, sits, drops the pages anyhow before him, and holds the backs of hands for a moment against his eyes. This morning we prolonged these activities, each of us waiting for something that was not quite right to right itself before we could begin. At last there was no putting it off any longer. Antonella had not arrived at her usual twenty-four minutes past eight, and she still hadn't arrived at eight-thirty. We set to work in an atmosphere that had been breached. It was as if one whole wall of the apartment had been torn away and was open to grey, slow-moving clouds.

By some odd co-incidence Antonella had arrived yesterday with a bunch of daffodils, which have just begun appearing in the florist's pails, and had set them, six in all, pale yellow trumpets above pale stems, in a tumbler from the kitchen. Flowers are not forbidden exactly – no one has thought to make provision against them – but they are unusual. They sat blaring on Antonella's desk, a reminder; and through their round mouths our lives were suddenly exposed to the spring and its changes, among which Antonella had abruptly disappeared.

Then, just a few minutes late, her key in the lock, and I waited expectantly for her breathless whistling as she hung up her cloak and stopped a moment before the hall mirror to fluff her hair.

Nothing. It was a tall boy with square eyebrows and a beard, his arms half out of a dufflecoat as he introduced himself: 'I'm Angelo.'

We stared. Enzo at last got up and shook the boy's hand, and the rest of us, in a dream, followed.

So it was true. Antonella had been called or replaced. The boy grinned, coughed, looked about to see which of the desks was unoccupied, and we watched as he turned his key, Antonella's key, in the drawer of the filing cabinet. It was empty. Someone had already removed the documents she was working on and everything relating to her.

By mid-morning the newcomer, Angelo, had been absorbed; that is, we had come to terms with the way he filled (with his intense stillness) the gap left by Antonella's everlasting whistling. When the time came to break for lunch he carried off the glass with Antonella's daffodils and set it, very carefully, on the dining room sideboard, a public place where it will no longer cast its shadow on the new set of documents he is at work on and will no longer be Antonella's.

His hands, I notice, are long and thin, with curly black hair on the back of the fingers and grease under the nails. When he eats he holds his knife like a pencil.

A mechanic of some sort, maybe an explosives man. He seems immediately at home among us. It is we who remain disturbed.

Is it always like this, I wonder, the first break in the group, or was Antonella special? Would I miss Carla or Arturo in the same way? I hadn't realized how completely the presence of the others has become part of my sense of myself during these weeks, how much my feeling of wholeness has been this plural existence and inter-dependence of all five. Now that one point of the star has been changed I am changed as well. I have to rethink a whole segment of myself.

Walking home I try to catch a glimpse of the headlines on a newsboard, but it is too soon. We are forbidden to buy papers or listen to the radio or watch TV, though I cheat a little, sometimes, by stopping at a bar to drink coffee while the news plays high up in a corner. Tonight I haven't the daring. I eat quickly and go straight to a movie.

Two girls from nowhere, a blond and a redhead, appear at the side of a motorway and are given a lift by a football team travelling to an away game in another town. Multiple sex on the bus while the highway landscape streams past. More sex in the dressing-room among open lockers; in the showers; in a steam-room with tiled walls. The girls are always naked. The football players wear their boots and a red and white striped jersey, and once one of the girls has a jersey, number 7: the passes and combinations a kind of off-the-field game.

I leave just before the end, take a bus to a quarter on the other side of town and find a girl.

14

I am intolerably restless. The disappearance of Antonella, though I ought to have been prepared for it, continues to disturb me. I know it is meant to happen like this, that she should simply vanish and become one again of the fifty-six million of whom one knows nothing; but it disturbs me just the same, and her replacement by Angelo, the munitions expert, with his thin fingers and lantern jaw, seems too hard a lesson. It is as if the organization had power not only to spirit us away but to transform us as well.

We are all changed by this: the weights between us have been subtly redistributed.

Carla minus Antonella is a lesser woman altogether. The addition of the bomb expert to her character, to her presence even, has shifted some delicate balance that makes her seem suddenly too cool, too hard, has given, by example perhaps, a grimmer line to her jaw and a whip-like emphasis to her gestures that goes beyond precision and makes everything she does seem over-dramatized.

As for Enzo, the removal from the star of one female

point and the introduction of another male one has been too much for him. His hostility to the newcomer is manifest, he cannot control it; and out of irritation with himself for giving so much away, for having in Angelo's case made a distinction, he has increased his hostility to Arturo and me as well. Mealtimes are aglow with tension, with palpable silences in which the bomb expert works his jaw, chewing every mouthful twenty times and leaving the sticky print of his fingers over everything he touches, quite unaware of what he has done to us.

He is, most of all, the one among us who has never known Antonella; that is what makes him so deeply a stranger. There is a whole side of us that he will never understand. Soon, I suppose, we will have to think of the group as reconstituted and take him into our lives as we took her, but somehow I don't fancy the aspects of myself that he might call into being. Why, I wonder? Is it the grease? That visible sign that we are not, after all, dealing entirely with abstracts, we clean-fingered intellectuals, but with a world in which reality has another shape and smell altogether?

There are also his long absences in the Signora's bedroom, where he is constructing a 'device'. At any moment, should those slim fingers make an error, we might be blown to smithereens. *That* is the shape of reality.

I must be chosen next. It angers me that I adjust so slowly. If Carla were to go now, or even Enzo or Arturo, I might break completely.

And that too is the 'shape of reality'.

15

Yesterday, for the first time, I had an encounter with one of my neighbours. The whole thing was simple enough, and might have been expected, but has added to my sense of unease. Another breach in my perfect isolation from the world about me.

Each of the various rooms and apartments in the palace has a post-box in the courtyard with a switch that lights the stairs above. I was making my way up beyond the first floor when I heard a whimpering to my right and then a faint voice: 'Please, whoever it is, I am here in the dark.'

I took a step or two into the corridor and hesitated. Better really not to get involved, to ignore the voice and go on.

'Please. I can't find my way up or down.' The voice was old and urgent. 'I can't sit here all night.'

It was just after six and still perfectly light outside, but on the stairway above as black as midnight.

'I've been here for hours.'

I took three or four paces along the corridor and realized I was at the foot of yet another stairway. The voice was immediately above. I took out my lighter. Half-sitting, half-sprawled on the stairs was an old woman in black, her shawl pushed back off her head, a brown-paper bag in her arms that had already split and spilled some of its contents: two lemons, a frozen chicken on a plastic tray, a head of lettuce. I knelt to gather them up and she grasped my hand with a strength that surprised and alarmed me.

'You won't leave me.'

'Of course not.' I took the paper bag, put the fallen articles back inside and drew it together as well as I could. 'Is it up here?'

'Yes. I got halfway up but the lights went out, the bulb must have blown. I couldn't see where I was. I tried to come down again,' she suddenly burst into tears, 'and fell.'

'Well, let's try again. I'll use my lighter.'

I soon lost all sense of what part of the palace we were in as we climbed stairway after stairway. 'Yes, yes,' she prompted me, 'to the right. Now left. We're almost there. Now the stairway at the end, I'm sorry to be so slow, but I'm old you know. Seventy-seven, and Celeste is eighty-two. I've lived here for fifty-four years. I came as a bride.' I had stopped and turned, holding the lighter high so that she could see her way, and she must have caught the look in my eyes, 'Oh yes,' she said, time goes fast enough,' as if fifty years were no more than the little space of darkness between us. She was holding up her key. We had come to the door. I stood back, with the parcel awkwardly in one hand and the lighter in the other so that she could open it.

'I'm coming, Celeste,' she called as she stooped to the keyhole, 'I'm coming, my darlings. I was lost on the stairs, but a kind young man has brought me back.'

We were in a good-sized vestibule. I suppose I had expected a cupboard like my own room, so the size of the entrance, its height, the oriental rugs, the mirror in its gilded frame, surprised me. 'Come,' she said, and turned left through a set of double doors into a sitting-room that must, I realized, run the whole length of the palace above the square. Its long windows with their gauze curtains and velvet drapes were filled with the western light off the river, a muted gold.

I had never seen a room like it. Every available space was filled with birdcages of every shape and size, squares, hexagons, spheres, some like pagodas, others again like mosques; all the birds chirping and shrilling and rolling and fluttering their coloured wings against the bars. I stood there, hugging my parcel with its one frozen chicken, and was dizzy with it all, the colour, the noise. Some of the birds in the cages, I now saw, were stuffed; and there were birds of more exotic varieties, with scarlet or bright blue wings, on the mantelpiece and under glass domes on table-tops. Coming in out of the dark maze of the stairway was like stumbling suddenly into a jungle clearing. Except for the clocks. There were also clocks: tall grandfathers in walnut and mahogany, inlaid or plain, with painted dials and wheels, chains, pendulums; slim grandmothers suspended; standing pieces in gilt and porcelain, their globes supported by naked nymphs or eighteenth-century shepherds; carriage clocks, water-clocks, clocks with a mechanism that went up and down like a sewing-machine needle, all ticking and tinkling. It was, I decided later, the mixture of shrill birdsongs and the unsynchronized ticking and chiming of the clockworks that most unnerved me – I couldn't imagine what kind of collector could have mixed them all up like this, the alive and the mechanical. It seemed profoundly crazy. And the thought that it had been here all along, just metres away from my own room, changed the whole place for me. The plainness of my cell seemed violated by the proximity.

The old woman had simply disappeared.

But was there, after all, behind a Chinese screen that was also covered with birds, made of *papier mâché* but stuck all over with natural feathers.

'Please,' she called, 'sit down somewhere, and make yourself at home. I'll be with you' – she paused and seemed to be lifting a heavy weight – 'in just a minute.'

She emerged wheeling another old woman in a chair.

'This is my sister-in-law, Celeste. Signora Carola, my husband's sister.' She took the parcel from me, looked about, frowned, and finally set it down under a sofa table.

'This is the young man who rescued me, Celeste. I'm about to give him a drink.'

The old woman in the chair made no sign of understanding.

She poured a glass and handed it to me. 'Poor

Celeste, she doesn't hear. But I feel it is mean not to tell her things. There! Your health! She does hear sometimes, I think. At least the birds. They're hers, you know, and the clocks were my husband Ugo's, he collected them from all over, England, the United States, Hungary. I've always hated them, and to tell you the truth, I don't care much for the birds either – I call them my darlings out of habit, for her sake. They have to be fed special kinds of seed and their cages have to be cleaned – a terrible business! You wouldn't believe what they manage to drop, those tiny creatures, in spite of the singing. Especially now that Pia doesn't come. Pia came even after we couldn't really pay her any more, but she's dead now, and her daughter came once or twice but couldn't bear the birds, so she stopped. I understand that. She didn't mean to be unkind. At least the clocks don't need to be fed or cleaned up after. But they do need winding. I hate the noise they make, but I couldn't bear it if they stopped and just sat there with all their works going to rust. So you see what my life is. I'm needed every minute. I go out only to get food . . .'

Outside in the dark of the stairway at last I began the difficult process of finding my way back to the point where my own stairway led off to the other side of the courtyard. It must have taken me nearly a quarter of an hour of false turnings and experimental steps along deserted corridors before I arrived at the wide passageway on the first floor. All this in absolute silence. The doors I passed were closed, and no sound penetrated their solid timber. They were all double-barred with that peculiar system of rising rods that is used against unwanted intruders. You see people standing at a door, turning their keys, once left, twice right, and listening for the mystical rising and falling within of the oiled machinery.

This glimpse into the life beyond one of those doors has thrown the whole palace into a new light. I had thought of my own room as hanging up there detached and in darkness, arrived at by its own set of stairways and utterly sealed off. Now it is part of a system that also contains, just below and to the right, on the other side of the courtyard, that room filled with clocks and songbirds, and the two old women.

I think of this encounter as being the first of my 'dreams' – a dream that I cannot interpret. The fact is that till then my nights in that little box of a room had been mostly dreamless, as if my sleep reflected the blankness of its walls, the absence from it of all but the most essential objects, and even those, as far as possible, impersonal. These last nights have been not troubled exactly, but coloured by extraordinary fantasies. I remember nothing afterwards, but the slight sweat on my skin when I wake, a lingering light behind the eyes that is not of this season, or this hemisphere, suggest that I have been off in exotic places and have undergone unusual and unsettling adventures. An element of the unpredictable, that for weeks now I have kept deeply submerged, has forced its way to the surface. I am unwilling at times to lie down, turn off the light and expose myself to the vagaries, sometimes savage, sometimes I suspect merely ridiculous, of my own imagination.

I begin to understand a little what the Master calls 'The anti-Works'.

16

A dream:

I have brought no detail out of the dark; only the mood of it that still colours the edge of everything about me, a weather I find myself moving in all day.

No mere recounting of the events of a dream can reproduce for us the peculiar quality of its light or the emotion it floods us with; the events are nothing. So if I am to describe it now it cannot be through any reference to the dream itself. I shall describe instead a photograph I discovered recently in an old book, which has been taken in just such a light and whose figures – or perhaps it is simply their disposition in the frame – evoke for me the mood of what I dreamt, though I have erased completely its sequence of phantom events.

It is afternoon in the early twenties. On the rocks of a little cove, with a low headland beyond and a path across it that leads perhaps to a village, five figures are waiting for a boat. The light comes over the smooth water from the direction in which they are gazing; there are big rocks made jagged with sun and shadow, and smaller rocks that barely break the ripples, on one of which, far out to the left of the photograph and completely surrounded by water, a girl is standing. She wears a silk dress in the flat-chested, beltless style of the period; it is dark with white spots. Her head is contained in a tight cloche, her hands are clasped below her waist and she is leaning backward a little to keep her balance, so that you are aware of the tension behind the knees and the effort it must take to keep her small feet firmly planted in the low-cut, strapped and buttoned shoes.

Deeper in the photograph, immediately behind her, a pleasant, well-knit young man is seated on one of the largest rocks of all, looking very casual in rolled shirt-sleeves. His collar has been unbuttoned and his tie hangs in a deep loop. One leg is comfortably raised to provide a rest for his elbow. His face is in profile. He too, like the girl, is looking towards the source of light, but her figure, in its tenseness, suggests that the boat is already in sight, she is prepared for embarkation and departure; he is still resting lazily in the sun, he sees nothing as yet. They might be present at different events.

Behind the girl again, but closer to the foreground, so that the lower part of his body is hidden by rocks, is an older man (nearing forty) in a cloak, or a topcoat drawn loosely about his shoulders. He wears a white panama with the brim turned down, round spectacles and a floppy cravat. His elbows are bent, his hands joined; he might be holding a ticket. His cloak suggests some other season than the one the girl has prepared for in her light silk dress, or the one the young man has loosened his tie and rolled his shirtsleeves to enjoy the warmth of. He belongs to another period, another class, another mode of life. What boat, one wonders, could be stopping off here to take all three of these passengers aboard? What journey could they be taking in common?

Higher up the shoreline, behind the formal stranger, stands another girl. She is wearing the same kind of clothes and shoes as the first, but everything about her is heavier, darker – and it isn't simply that she is further from the left-hand side of the photograph which is so brightly suffused with sunlight. The thick plait over her shoulder, her stance, the strap bag that takes the weight of her bent arm, her flesh – all these are dark; she is standing in the light of a different occasion, so that her face can barely be seen, and she is looking not out to sea, in the direction of the picture's expected action, but has half-turned, as if momentarily distracted, to where, behind us, some other event is in process, some other conveyance has appeared. (Is it a fishing-boat? A space-ship?) She is younger than the others, she might be seventeen, and the shape of her face – she is too deep in shade to have features – suggests that she is extraordinarily pretty.

There is one other figure. Seated a little apart from the rest, on the rocks at the far right of the photograph, and facing dead ahead so that his face is in shadow, is a young peasant. He wears a suit, a tie, a flat tweed cap, and he sits with his forearms extended along his thighs. Only the big fists are in full sunlight. The grain

110

of the material in the flat cap that is set straight on his brow, in the jacket that fits tight over the square shoulders, is so clear that you could pick out the threads; but his face is in total darkness and his fists are a blaze.

There is nothing in the photograph, save perhaps the isolation of the figures from one another, that could account for the immense sadness it fills me with. The sun is shining, the afternoon sky makes the pale sea shimmer. It is a sadness that seems inevitable, and to be in the very nature of things. Fifty years ago it had these five strangers looking, at this moment, towards the arrival of a boat that may or may not have appeared, that may or may not be making towards the rocks of the little cove, out of a future that has, for long years now, been no more than a moment in the past. They seem just close enough to look like contemporaries, and just distant enough to be touched with the unlikeliness of those who belong already to history. I find myself fingering the surface of the photograph and being surprised that the rocks are not jagged, that the roughness of that boy's jacket, which the light inside the photograph makes so real, cannot be felt.

My dream stands in the same relationship to me as the photograph. It teases me with the deepest and most physical sense of space, light, weather, of the various textures of things, of a huge and inevitable sadness, but when I try to enter its reality I cannot. Is this what the dead feel?

17

There are times, in spite of our orders, when it is difficult to shut out the news. A few words overheard in the bus are like the turning of a shocking page.

Another nest discovered and the terrorists taken with all their documents – any one of which, together with a hundred other seemingly unrelated facts, might throw up as in a puzzle, where it needs only the slightest rearrangement of the coloured squares to produce a pattern that is instantly recognizable, a name, a face.

Or a shoot-out in a suburban apartment. A quiet corridor in the middle of the night runs red with blood. One, two, five bodies, called up without warning out of the depths of sleep, fully armed but dressed only in underpants and singlet or in the briefest slip, go down in a storm of bullets before any one of them can pull the pin on a grenade or fire off a single shot, stepping straight out of the warmth and safety of sleep into their own blood.

All this one must imagine from facts picked up here and there between talk about hair-styles, boyfriends and last night's television programmes – gossip from the front, filled out with newspaper headlines on windy boards and images it is better not to look at, flickering high up in the corner of a bar or repeated five times over, in sickening colour, on the display sets in shop windows.

This, three days after Antonella's disappearance, is how I hear of the gun-battle at T.

Three comrades caught in a car and surrounded, all three killed. The driver instantly, shot at the wheel; the other man in a brief exchange of gunfire from behind the door of the vehicle; the girl in a side street as she tries to get away, sprawling in the gutter with her skirt up over one thigh and a shoe missing.

There are pictures. They are terribly distorted, the figures already dissolving as they move quickly on out of life. With their edges frayed, great holes for eyes, they have been endowed with a fuzzy insubstantiality, a flat black-and-white quality that marks them as figures from the news, fighters at the edge of history who have, as it were, broken up in casting themselves against solid print.

Newspaper photography.

Far from catching life it disintegrates and dissolves it, first reducing it to a pattern of tiny dots and areas of patchy light and dark, then recreating it to make an image we recognize but no longer feel related to, something that belongs to 'the news', and in entering that utterly flat dimension relinquishes its right to be considered real.

Of course the acts we produce have significance

only if they are reported. But the very fact of their being reported changes them. As they pass into the public domain they lose whatever they had of flesh and blood and acquire that deadness, that finality, that impersonal and isolating distance that belongs to what has been given over to the tense of retelling: to history, to death. There is no way out of this dilemma. We can only work through a medium which is itself the enemy and whose very nature is to deprive whatever it reports of life and power.

One sees this most clearly when a cache of weapons is pictured on the same page as a group of comrades, either alive or dead. They look so solid, those Lugers, Skorpions, Smith and Wessons, grenades, anti-tank missiles, all laid out neatly in rows. It is the human figures that break up in the mind, that fail to hold their form. It is difficult, even with a real name supplied, to imagine that any of these figures might once have been more than what the pictures reduce them to, such obvious outsiders, rebels, misfits that you wonder how they ever went unrecognized in the streets.

No resemblance at all between Graziella da Soto, aged 20, Chilean, and the Antonella whose bubbly music so often distracted me and set my fingers tapping on the desk. These blank eye-sockets, these luminous cheeks, this raw mouth.

But it is her, it must be.

Graziella.

I buy a paper, take it back to my room and sicken myself with it, devouring every line.

Next day I am inclined to believe that I am the only

114

one of us who has cheated. But it is soon clear from the atmosphere as we set to work that the others are also dealing this morning with the huge clamour of Antonella's disintegration under the fire of five plain-clothes policemen in an ambush. The office is full of the sudden rackety burst of the machine-guns – five seconds of utter bedlam over and over in the silence of our skulls; and the flesh is solid enough to feel the impact, however subtly in the photographs it may suggest nothing more than light dots and dark. Only our mechanic seems unaware that we are in turmoil here, that all the conditions of our relationship to one another have once again been changed, and that some part of us still echoes with unresolved possibilities as the bullets tear through it in a last moment of con-sciousness.

Again next day the papers are full of it. More theories, different facts, but the same pictures.

I turn away from my neighbours on the bus and for the first time feel anger and disgust to see the dirty black print that comes off on their hands, on their eyes too, as they rub themselves against the obscene para-graphs. I stay out of the bars. I eat at home. One more day perhaps and something new will have arisen to wipe Antonella off the newsboards and the lips of the commuters – a plane-crash, a bribery scandal. She will remain in the public files, every detail of her existence lovingly recorded and remembered, and in the heads of Carla, Arturo, Enzo and me; and I see now that we will always be part of one another and will always feel the absence of the others, in whatever form, as the

115

aching of a phantom limb. I had not seen that till now. I find in myself a kind of tenderness, even for Enzo, who seems 'nobler' and more hostile than ever in this new light, and for Arturo too, who has had his hair cut and looks unbearably school-boyish. As for Carla, I dare not look at her. One glance between us and our whole lives might fly apart.

On my way home I stop in the cold and watch some children playing in the square, small muffled figures flying about over the gravel between the trees; one of them always the outsider, the others always in flight from him, but their cries, their trails of white breath, mingling and the outsider always managing at last to touch one of his comrades and so break back into the group.

I watch for ten minutes the ever-changing pattern with its simple rule, and for all that time am intensely absorbed and happy, caught up in the energy of those hot little bodies in their swinging away from whoever it is that is momentarily 'he', as the ambiguous gift of singularity, like a curse or infection, passes from one to another and they find themselves in flight from a different centre, throwing their slight weight off now in a fresh direction and leaving behind always, under the wet branches, the quick-fading white of their breath.

18

On my desk this morning, along with a new instalment of the 'Work in Progress' and two articles on the Master from American magazines (one on water as a regenerative symbol in his novels, the other a painful attempt to define his political attitudes) a cutting from one of the provincial papers. Three brief paragraphs.

They announce the death, in a clinic at P., of Signora Dora Cavani.

A well-known figure in the years between the wars, though now largely forgotten, she was, it seems, the friend, patroness and correspondent of some of the most famous artists of the century – among them, in a list that includes Stravinski, De Chirico, Saba, Pound, Pavese and Kurt Schwitters, our author. She has been in a coma, kept alive by a life-support system, for the past six weeks, and is to be buried from the Church of Sant' Agostino at three-thirty on Tuesday afternoon.

So there it is: the day, the time. The jigsaw is complete. Tucked away in the announcement of a death in a provincial paper, the final piece.

I read the cutting a dozen times over and can hardly believe it.

From the very beginning one of the puzzles to me has been how our people could be certain that the great man, who goes nowhere these days, never leaves the house or breaks his routine, would appear in the piazza for his own assassination.

But there was never any doubt of it. The thread we have been hanging on all these weeks was the woman's life. Laid out there between white walls in the clinic at P., it was her shallow breathing that determined the time-span of our operations, and her feeble heartbeat, sustained by a machine whose little wheels turned night and day and whose needle recorded, under the eyes of anxious monitors, her fragile hold on her own life, that held me off and kept him safe.

I had often conceived of some secret link between us as we sat absorbed in our different tasks; he at the big desk above the fields, in a room still coloured by the light of his dreams, I at my table in the apartment; isolated, alone, and with four hundred kilometres and a lifetime between us, but gathered in the same fateful design.

Now, in retrospect, I must add another to the picture: the woman – prone, gaunt, flat-chested, her mouth slightly open to take in air; and beyond even her, the machine to which all three of us were obscurely connected, its metal surfaces softly agleam as it marked its own time in the dark.

It makes another pattern altogether, and I should

have learned nothing in these long weeks of immersing myself in his world of delicate distinctions and balances if I did not feel, at this moment, how clumsy a third I make, intruding so crudely, armed only with a cause and cold steel, on a relationship that has been sustained with so much tact, and such high feeling on both sides, for more than half a century. I am abrupt, accidental. She has been, for all that long stretch of time, the keystone of his existence.

Dora Cavani.

The name echoes and re-echoes in his papers. There are nearly a thousand letters to her, from Switzerland and Argentina during his exile, from his travels all over the Mediterranean in the thirties – vivid, hastily scribbled postcards or deep meditations, one or two even from the days when he was a student in Milan, before his gift had reached out and claimed him. They are not passionate; she was, after all, happily married to another man. But he dedicated a volume of essays to her, and she has sometimes been thought to be the model for Renata in an early story of first love, though the story's hero is his brother. (Is there a clue there to something deeper than he has ever confessed?) It has been suggested that his return to P., twelve years ago, may be linked with her retirement there on the death of her husband. She is certainly the Dear Friend he so often apostrophises in the later essays, the last survivor of an earlier world with whom he can share his memories, and through whose sympathy and affection so much of it comes back to him – as he has put it, 'another patch of blue'. Is she also, perhaps, the

119

Dearly Beloved whose identity the commentators have never established but whose presence he so often evokes as Guide and Muse, the one true love he has never outgrown? Was it her presence at P., rather than the recovery of his own deepest roots of family, place, language, that let him through again into his earliest childhood – or are the two things, as he felt them, indistinguishable?

A long passage in the *Memoir* describes an accidental return to the district, and a walk from the farmhouse where he had grown up to the house of an early love, an hour off over the hills. The walk, as so often with him, immediately becomes symbolic, and the more so as he notes, rock by rock, leaf by leaf, each landmark along the way, re-entering, as it were, the strong net of feelings that for years had lain over these objects. Having for so long retained their power, they now, as he approaches, release it again as if nothing had changed: a line of poplars along a fence, all the trunks black, the leaves bright gold; five stepping stones over a stream, the third of which is not quite firm – and just as he had remembered after nearly sixty years, it tilts underfoot; a lilac bush in a clump of ferns. All the feelings inherent in the landscape come back with instant force, but he understands them now as he had failed to understand before. It is his younger self who stands looking back across the whole stretch of his life, and his younger self who starts breathlessly up the slope towards the house, where the young girl still stands under the jasmine bush at the end of the path, though it is – O happy rediscovery! – an older woman who turns and makes towards him.

So he found his way back, he tells us, to the beginning, 'a full circle to the place where I began.'

I had assumed all this was only half true: a grain of actuality – how large no one could tell – the rest an elaboration. It had seemed too deeply stained with poetry to be true to the events.

But there is a poetry of events after all. Think of what is now to occur. It makes a pattern he would recognize and approve as being very much his own. A touch more melodramatic, that death on the steps after the Beloved's funeral, than he might allow himself in fiction, but as true to the real shape of his life as anything he could have imagined, an ending that richly justifies everything he has ever claimed for himself. Mightn't he even, in some obscure way, have chosen it? Or imagined it deep within him and then used his extraordinary powers to bring it about?

And what part do I play in all this? Might I, facing him on the steps of the piazza, revolver in hand, be just what he had already foreseen? And I don't mean the assassin of Santo Domingo. Or if I do, I mean him only as a shadow of what we might both be: the brother fallen in battle nearly sixty years ago and returning at last to claim his life, the son with his rifle, who aims at some distant object, then, with a knowing smile, turns it squarely upon himself, and for a second time finds his father's heart. Will he meet me as a figure entirely known and expected? – 'Ah yes, it is you. I should have guessed.' – conjured up in the piazza, at the last moment, out of his need to complete

121

the business after his own wishes and in his own style.

It occurs to me that I will only make sense of all this by going back to the works themselves and reading them through again from first to last. Somewhere in the slow unfolding of his life in time is the pattern this new piece of evidence may reveal to me. I need to see that pattern. Not for what it will explain of our author, or the mysterious wholeness and poetry of his life, but to discover what I am doing here and whose destiny it is I have been summoned to fulfil.

But there is no time. I have been handed this last piece of the jigsaw when it is too late to use it. I will enter the piazza as the figure in this drama who knows least of all what it really means. My researches were for nothing. I had the evidence before me but did not know what I was looking for. I was looking for *him*. I ought all the time to have been seeking myself.

19

It has come. Returning to my room this evening I had the clear sensation, before I had even felt for the switch, that its order had been disturbed. There on the table, the only surface in the room that wasn't perfectly bare, lay a squat, brown-paper parcel. I stood mesmerized before it.

It was shapeless, and might have contained anything: a spanner or a child's tip-truck or a shaving kit. A moment later, with no memory of having untied the string or unfolded the three thicknesses of paper, I was holding in my hand, and so easily that I might have handled this thing every day of my life, a ·765 Beretta automatic.

I had asked myself many times how the order would arrive. I suppose I expected a knock on the door and a face, a voice at last, someone who might put his hand on my shoulder and offer a few words of gentle reassurance – I wouldn't have had to believe them, the voice would be enough – maybe wish me luck even or make some kind of awkward joke.

Not at all. The angel of this annunciation is black,

cold, and fits snugly into the hand.

No need for words. The object is itself the message. I have known from the beginning that when the sign is made I must present myself at a certain place at a certain time and wait to be picked up.

So it is fixed. These last weeks are already done with. I am turned in the direction of what my life is to be from now on. But before that, there is the brief detour to the Piazza Sant' Agostino at P.

Now that it has come I feel light-headed and suddenly very tired. I lay the weapon down, without bothering to rewrap it or make any other preparations, stretch full length on the bed and immediately fall into a profound sleep.

Total blackness, as if I had been drugged.

When I wake hours later the light is still on. The clock says five minutes to three. I lie staring at the ceiling, and for the first time since the wrappers revealed the shiny glint of it, my mind begins working again and my heart suddenly thumps and races. I go quickly to the table. It is there: utterly itself. Black, weighty, its clean lines, with the inviting grip, so beautifully attuned to its purpose that the purpose itself seems like nature; it is as if such an object had existed from the first moment of creation, and the hand, its four fingers and flexible thumb, had grown to fit it, the two shapes, hand and pistol, developing in perfect parallel with one another to reach their perfected forms.

Only my hand is shaking too badly at the moment to take it up. I bite my lip, clench my fists at the table edge, wait for my blood to settle. When my hand is steady I reach out for it. The grip of the thing, its balance, its coolness, has a soothing effect, such as I might have expected from that reassuring voice, for which it is after all the impersonal substitute. I stand in the centre of the room and hold it easily just at waist level. I have regained that unconscious, almost dream-like self that unwrapped the parcel and let the gun settle so snugly into place. That is how it must be later. As it is now.

Meanwhile there are preparations to make.

I wash and change my clothes, then arrange my few possessions in a haversack. I do all this very slowly, very carefully, to fill the time; and discover that for the past ten minutes or more I have been talking aloud though I can't recall a word that has been said. When everything is neatly done, and every last trace of my presence has been removed from the room, I sit on the bed and wait.

The room contains no trace of me.

I remove myself from it.

An hour later I start awake where I have sunk back against the wall, perfectly alert and clear-headed, fully dressed even to the jacket, and with the haversack, in which the gun is hidden, already over my shoulder. It is after four.

Now begins the worst of it. I have nothing to do but wait. I am not required for several hours yet, but here I am with my whole life on my hands and a mind that has thrown off weariness and the first shock that laid me out like a hammerblow, and is simply with me now as it always is, a machine with a life of its own and all the past available in its memory banks to be called as needed, and set for a future it never doubts for a moment is there. The mind imposes itself. It too has to be taken along and out through the event. Meanwhile I would give anything for some fact or puzzle with which it might occupy itself and leave me free . . .

I find I have been talking aloud again, and again there is no record in my memory of the conversation; or if there is I cannot locate it. Maybe it will reappear later, in what I have already set my course for, and want now with a passionate longing – that ordinary life that lies just a few hours ahead, on the far side of the event.

Yes, I tell my father, as if picking up the threads of a broken conversation, *I do mean to marry. Yes, grandchildren. Your grandchildren. Mine.*

My body knows them, those future generations as if the years to come lay vividly before me and they were already flesh and blood, filling the silence with their voices. I would like to call out to them, but have forgotten their names.

I wish you were here, I say. *I want so much at this moment to talk to you, to let my mind idle on the vibrations of your voice, to have that set the tone of these last moments in the room.*

And realize, with a little shock, that it isn't my father I am addressing but *him*.

Is he stirring already out of the shallow sleep of the old? Turning towards the first light of dawn that I can see colouring the window, pushing a foot down into the colder reaches at the bottom of the bed, snuffling, hauling the rug up over his hunched shoulder, rising slowly towards the surface, the few pints of thin blood still pumping, the viscera tightly packed under the wrinkled belly, still miraculously intact after another night out there in the no-man's-land of sleep? This, I feel, might be the moment. Just now in the lightness of his early morning sleep, when the mind looks two ways, we might make contact at last and the conversation take place that I long for as one might long for forgiveness. It is after all *words* that I need. I feel so utterly alone, so vulnerable to things: to the little waterdrops that will be hanging on the bare twigs of trees in the square below, little swellings of early light where next month there will be blossom; to the children with their pale cries that I stood and watched playing tag in the square, who will be deep now in the sleep of early childhood or making those fabulous excursions out of themselves that are children's dreams; to the cats scavenging for scraps in cold doorways; to the shallow pools of rain in the gravel walks that will be dry by midday, their drying up a process of forgetting, drop by drop, the passage of the new moon across them; to the grains of soot that settle on treetrunks and boughs, leaving them streaked with dew; to the round lids of manholes that are stamped with the city's ancient insignia – a blind eye turned downward into the bowels of the city, whose odours clog it with rust; to the light that slowly advances out of the darkness of things, out of leaves, stones, pools, scraps of paper, out of hands and faces, out of the depths of space itself, and which cannot be resisted as it pours out endlessly, endlessly, giving each thing shape, colour, solidity, making reality something that knocks against all five senses to prove us real. At this point of powerful weakness, of openness to the common life of things, surely we might at last make contact.

I feel him turn once more. He is at the very edge of wakefulness now, but troubled still by the tail of a dream that detains him down there, though the small sounds of morning are already providing the threads on which he will rise and break surface.

His hand goes out to the waterglass on the night table with the pills beside it. *Why am I thinking of that young man – that seminarist, Francesco, who killed the ambassador at Santo Domingo? Why after all this time has he come back to tug at me? I've said all I had to say about him, or for him. All I knew.* In this odd moment between sleep and waking he almost catches sight of me, might still, if he could grasp the fading vision at the corner of his eye – *that young man, was it? at the tramstop in Zurich* – see me here as he sits up and swings his legs over the side of the bed, with his bluish feet not yet thrust into the black kid slippers. *I have woken early.*

I wait, listening. The thin lips move. The head nods over its thought, or perhaps simply because its weight is no longer quite controllable. But there is no word. In a moment his daughter will appear, place a dedicatory kiss on his brow, express surprise that on this of all days – later, in the afternoon he has an appointment – he has beaten the clock and stirred early. Yes, there is her tap at the door.

She leaves his coffee on the tray and goes into the next room. As he sips and takes a bite from his English water-biscuit he consults the pad that stands beside the glass of water and reads the scribblings that have emerged out of his broken sleep, the night-thoughts that offer the merest, most fascinating glimpse – just the end of a page tantalizingly lifted – of 'the anti-Works', those shadows, volume by volume, of what he has brought into the light. No clue there. What was it that was haunting him? *What? What?*

I am already fading from view. The possibility will pass. He is already engaged, his mind suddenly active in one of the scribblings. He adds something. Crosses a word out and adds two more. Is it some thought to be discovered on the nightpad that gives his mouth that little twist as he takes another sip from the cup, or just the bitterness of the coffee, which he takes without sugar? *Ah, the world is so strange, so sad! But interesting!*

Too late now. He has already abandoned me. If there was a point, back there, when his mind, not yet grounded in actualities and particulars, was adrift among the infinite possibilities and still open for any one of them to enter or be entered, it has passed. His working day has begun.

He puts the coffee aside, still unfinished, and scribbles rapidly, making a little chuckling sound. His eyes brighten. Another fragment of darkness has been brought out into the world of grace and light.

These are the only words that emerge. I cannot read them.

It is seven-thirty. The water is still running for his bath. I go out quickly without looking at the room where I have spent nearly six weeks of my life, close the door softly, descend the stairs, pass the corridor that leads to my old lady with the clocks, which will be ticking away now as they set out across the morning, and the caged birds in the dark of their covers, not yet pricked into song.

I cross the square. It is empty, except for a tramp curled up as usual in the doorway of the florist's. I turn into the avenue, walk briskly to the corner and then run the last twenty metres.

I am on my way.

20

It is over, and nothing has gone as planned.

The car, when it pulled in under the archway where I had been instructed to wait, was a delivery wagon with a girl at the wheel, a girl with sleek black hair that curled outwards under her ears. It was only when I climbed in beside her and she turned to smile at me that I recognized her. Carla! How different the change of hair colour made her. I opened my mouth to speak, but before I could do so she introduced herself.

'I'm Adriana. I'm to drive you. I am also your cover. It isn't forbidden, but it would be better if we didn't speak.'

We drove out of the narrow street into a wider one, then out along one of the viales, and within minutes the town, all its church towers picked out in the early sunlight, was hovering below, caught in gaps between the trunks of pines.

I glanced sideways once at her profile and she tilted her head a little and gave me a clear indication that that too, though it wasn't exactly forbidden, might be better avoided. I watched the town, which I had never really got to know in my five weeks there, sink away between the rough-textured pink and brown trunks – its great dome, its famous galleries with all the paintings at this hour still in darkness behind locked doors, its river spanned by elegant stone bridges. But at last it was gone and there were stone walls close on either side, with just a glimpse of olive-groves or orchards on the rises and Carla's unfamiliar profile under the black wig.

It disturbed me to know that the girl beside me had once stepped into my sleep and played a part there that I could never quite recall, though my body remembered, with a rising warmth, the mood of it. Had she been dark-haired then as well? It seemed to me now that she had, and that it was this, rather than anything we had said or done, that had embarrassed me in the days afterwards when I met her eyes across the dining table; as if I had hit upon some aspect of her in my sleep that she might not be aware of, or had long kept hidden, as she once, and quite consciously, had brought out some hidden side of me, when standing before the mirror in the apartment she had touched my cheeks with make-up and put those little dots of scarlet at the corners of my eyes. Now here she was just as I had imagined her. Or had my dream itself been changed in recollection by her new appearance? Our relationship has always, it seems, been closer than we knew. Week after week we have been engaged on the same material, covering one another in secret, working side by side in separation but endlessly crossing tracks. Is that why I dreamed of her, and so precisely as she now appeared? Not blond Carla, but Carla Adriana in a black wig. And what, I wondered, given my own involvement, was her relationship with our famous victim? What aspects of herself had she been following in the vast mirror-world of his writings and how was her part in it related to mine? Once again it occurred to me that I needed to read the whole works through again, this time seeking her, my understudy, my double in another form.

She turned her head once or twice to observe me. (Had I been talking aloud?) And this time it was I who obeyed the rules.

'We've got about four hours of this,' she said, as we pulled away from the toll-gate on the highway. 'You should try to sleep.'

I might have protested then that I had slept enough, and was already in what seemed to myself to be too trance-like a state for what lay ahead. But her words, spoken I thought later as one might speak to a small child, had the effect on me of a hypnotic command. Perhaps it was the warmth of the cabin and the protective closeness of her presence: perhaps it was simply the steady motion of the vehicle, or my own wish to be released for a time from my condition of questioning anxiety; but almost immediately I began to lose consciousness, felt her settle a cushion under my head, and fell into a blankness that only gradually lightened, after I don't know how long, to reveal a long flat stretch of beach in what I recognized as Southern California. It was mid-afternoon. Fog lay over the ocean, but the beach and the very edge of the sea were in sunlight. Small clean waves fell over themselves on the glassy sand, and half a dozen riders were urging their horses through them, the horses, with highlights shifting on their flanks, tall and dark against the sky, the riders straight and tall, but faceless. Their voices urged the horses on with clouds of white; and slowly, one after another, the horses turned seaward, waded out with the strange light on their flanks and were lost in fog. And it was as if I were one of those horses; or maybe a rider who had slipped from his horse far out. Warm water was all about me but I was in fog. There was no sign of the shore and no indication out there of where it might lie or in which direction I should strike out towards it. The water was thick and warm, and I had the sick sensation that if the fog were to lift and light fell upon it, it would be red. I struggled and it began to thicken, my limbs were clogged. I worked my legs and shoulders, I tried to cry out, and the air in my lungs was raw and cold. I tried again, and this time my throat was filled with sound. A cry spun out. It was a lifeline I could grasp, hold and climb out on.

I blinked awake. We had come to a halt.

'You were having a bad dream,' Carla Adriana told me, once again as if she were explaining something to a very young child. There was a touch of anxiety in her tone that might have said: 'You need watching. You could make a botch of this. You've got too much imagination. That's why I am here. Not everyone, you know, needs a cover.' But she didn't say that. What she said was: 'I've got a delivery to make. You can help if you like.'

134

She got out and went round to the doors of the van. The back was stacked with cases of apples and it was only now that I smelled them. We were parked in front of an open fruitshop that was also a bar, general store, phone-post and restaurant. Three or four tables without chairs stood in front of it, their white paint chipped with rust. I leaned into the van and took one of the boxes.

'No,' she told me, 'not that one. The one underneath. And be careful, it's heavier than you'd expect. I'll take the other one myself.'

We carried the two boxes through the empty shop into a passageway between the kitchen, which was deserted but clean, with all its metal surfaces polished, and two dirty lavatories, one of them without a door. A woman appeared from the rooms behind and Carla told her matter-of-factly: 'A delivery for Piero.' The woman nodded. 'No other message. Just the delivery and the fact that we called.' The woman, who was old, nodded again and drew a brown shawl around her shoulders. She was carrying a roll of grey knitting with enormous wooden needles plunged through the ball.

'Haven't you got time for coffee?'

'No,' Carla told her. 'We're not late but we haven't got time.'

The woman made a line with her lips. 'Good luck then.'

Carla stuck her hands deep into the pockets of her cardigan and lifted her chin in what I had always thought of as a haughty manner when she was a tall blond, but which now seemed merely nervous. It needed her darker appearance for me to see her as she really was. 'Come on,' she said, leading the way out.

She locked the back doors of the van, climbed in and we were soon speeding away again under the new spring leaves. 'If you want coffee,' she told me, 'there's a flask, and I brought sandwiches. I thought we'd stop and eat when we're further along the way.'

Two hours later, parked in a laneway off the main road, we ate ham rolls, drank a little white wine and had coffee. The rolls were wrapped in a linen tea-towel that was properly starched and ironed; there were paper napkins as well, paper cups for the wine and more for the coffee. But she had forgotten to bring sugar.

'Damn,' she said, 'damn, damn! How could I forget?' I had never seen her so disturbed. I thought of her admonishing God as she worked away with her rubber, eliminating errors, but the error this time was hers.

'Really, I don't mind at all,' I told her, sipping the bitter brew. 'I even prefer it.'

But my preferences, or my polite lies, were not the point. She had planned that everything down to the last detail should be right and her own forgetfulness upset her. It was more than a matter of bad housekeeping. It was as if some essential ingredient of the situation had been fatally overlooked, leaving a gap that could never be filled. If I could forget this, she seemed to say, I could forget anything. What is it that I have forgotten? She tried to taste what it was in the coffee, but it was not there.

When she started the car again it stalled. Another failure. She swore and seemed suddenly in a different mood. As if she had broken through out of one sort of weather into another, just as the day had with its lowering clouds and threat of rain. It occurred to me that to recover her earlier spirits she would have to push back the dark, close-fitting wig she wore and shake her blondness free. But of course it wasn't as simple as that. I recognized the thought as part of my own growing depression. The last station in our journey was past; there would be no more stops now before the final one. The little cabin, which four hours ago had been quite unfamiliar to me, had become a place I felt reluctant to leave. It was security. It was on the known side, the safe side of the event. And our meal together, which I had not thought about while we were eating it, was something I would gladly have gone back to savour: the crisp rolls, the whiteness of the tea-towel with its sharp creases, even the bitter coffee. They had, in retrospect, an importance, those shared moments of isolation together in the cabin, the food, the drink, that I ought to have lingered over, whereas I had simply accepted them and let them pass. 'Why,' I asked myself, 'do I understand things only when I am no longer part of them?' And that too depressed me. The change of weather in the cabin was all my own. That little business of the missing sugar might have affected Carla less than it affected me, and the wish that she would push back her wig and be Carla again was also for my sake, not hers. It would put us back in the safety of yesterday, or three hundred kilometres ago. I watched the numbers fall through the little window on the dashboard and was so mesmerized by them that I was hardly aware of the first drops of rain till we rode right into the storm, then out again into watery sunshine and shiny pavements, then into a longer stretch of it as we came to the outskirts of the town.

So I never did see what the place was like. We simply crawled along blind with our lights on, while headlamps and trees and misty soft-edged figures swarmed across the glass.

'We're almost there,' Carla Adriana said, peering over the curve of the wheel. 'I'll stop a moment under the arcades and we can have a cigarette. You'll hear the clock strike. Be sure to take everything with you.'

She was pushing her things, including the scraps of our picnic, into a leather shoulder-bag

'I'm to ditch the car in the parking lot in the next street. The car you are to look out for afterwards is a blue Renault with a local numberplate. It will be waiting at the corner, right beside the bank. The driver will take you to the edge of town and another car will take you on. Is all that clear?'

I nodded. She lit a cigarette and passed it to me, then lit another and threw her head back in the old way, drawing deep. We sat in silence.

I had expected in these last moments to have some power of control over myself; to close my eyes perhaps and count, or to think of one of those imaginary scenes that I had used as a child for putting myself to sleep and could still evoke on occasions, or even to find some formula of words, a poem, Ronsard's "Pour Hélène" which I had learned at highschool and which ever since had stayed irrelevantly in my head, or a prayer whose phrases could be repeated over and over till the time was filled. Instead I was invaded by blind panic and a hundred questions I wanted suddenly to put to Carla, not all of them by any means concerned with the matter in hand, and some of which she would be no more equipped to answer than I myself was. After all my weeks of preparation I was quite unready for what was to occur.

'Now.' she said. 'It's time.' She gave a quick glance at the rear vision mirror and started the motor. 'Go!'

I must have opened the door and stumbled out as I had earlier fallen asleep, simply on the authority of her voice, because almost instantly I was alone under the arcades, which were dripping after the storm. She was gone, and I was walking, with a dreamlike sense of everything having too sharp a focus, along the western edge of the piazza, past the unfrequented café and the shop that sells dress material and cushions.

The light was brilliantly clear, as it can be after a downpour and the square was full of pieces of sky with pigeons sipping at them or splashing up broken glass. A bell was tolling. People stood about with open umbrellas. Hot little raindrops were striking diagonally through the sunlight, and the façade opposite, which seemed un-nervingly close, too close for the square I had imagined, was luminous and golden, all its details hard-edged and precise as if newly carved.

It was like going back to a place of your childhood

and finding it familiar but wrong. All the dimensions were wrong. And I hadn't reckoned on the loudness of the bell or the shortness of the time it would take me to arrive at the platform, or, as the great central doors of the cathedral clanged and swung open, on the appearance right behind me of a uniformed beadle with a cocked hat and breeches, who stood for a moment before the open darkness where the doors had been with a wand held at arm's length before him and might have been about to knock three times for a performance to begin.

He stood, then lowered the wand in an exaggerated ceremonial fashion, and moved.

Behind him the priest and his acolytes in white linen. Behind them the coffin, on the shoulders of six uniformed ushers. Then at last the old man, looking so much more fragile than I had expected, a thin stooped figure with a skull like a baby's, almost transparent; you could see the blue veins in it, softly pulsing. He wore a morning coat and striped trousers and carried a shiny top hat. At his side the daughter, all in grey, had turned aside for a moment and was engaged in push-ing up a black umbrella. As I stepped forward she glanced up. *An extraordinary woman*, I thought as our eyes met. Then she looked down and her mouth opened in what must have been a cry. She had seen the gun.

Time stopped for whole seconds as we stood there, simply staring at one another. She seemed tremend-ous, awful. I had a sudden sick impression of the full weight of what it was – flesh, bone, a spirit of female power and protection – that had taken up residence in the grey figure and was about to interpose itself between me and what I must do, and of the forty-nine years in which she had been gathering herself for it. Her shoulders rose, a thick wad of muscle appeared in her neck. She prepared to charge. At some point years before I was born this moment must have presented itself as what her whole life was making for. She saw that now and launched herself towards me, a creature out of another order of existence, fully armed, resplendent, and fixing me with a fierce gaze as if to say, *There, you thought this moment was yours and that you would control it, but look, it is mine.* She was the embodiment, in grey silk, of everything I had tried to exclude from the event and had known all along could not be excluded. How could that be? I had known it and only now saw what I knew.

A bullet struck her in the shoulder. She seemed unaware of it. It was when the second bullet tore into her that she fell back, staggered, and stood still, then began, very slowly, to sink to her knees; but with immense slowness, and with a look of infinite surprise and disappointment, as if drawn down by a natural force that she had tried with all her being to resist but which was, after all, too strong for her. She was only human. The angelic powers had deserted her. She still held on to the umbrella, like a parachute by which she would not be saved.

I stood over her with the unsteady Beretta. One of her hands flapped against the flagstones, which were greasy with blood, and the sounds that came from her open mouth might have been in another tongue. I leant forward a little to try and catch them. 'Bgrrr,' she thundered, 'Tgrrr, dgrrrr, mgrrrr.!' One part of me was held fascinated with the effort of trying to translate, and I thought that if I closed my eyes and listened in the dark the words might make sense and reveal their meaning to me. But another part of me had already turned away. There was still the old man.

He had straightened and turned at the woman's first cry of alarm and he stood halted now, staring right at me. It was the third and fourth shot that struck him, once in the breast, once in the throat, and he went down immediately. The remaining shots went off at random, entirely without my will, and I heard them resounding behind me as I broke away into the open square in the direction of the fourth of my seven photographs, all rinsed and new in the sunlight, and saw in my path as the noise rolled away behind me, Carla, blond again and with a coat over her arm that must have concealed the second weapon. My first thought was that she was about to shoot me. The bell went on tolling, and as I swerved away her image was replaced by that of the woman with the umbrella. She was kneeling right in my path, her hands raised, her mouth open, and the terrible sound that came out of it, the long agonized cry of an animal wounded beyond comprehension, was my own voice crying over and over words that I understood only too well. 'No! No! No!', like the tolling of a bell. Of the moment I had so carefully prepared for, the luminous moment when he and I would stand face to face in the full understanding of what was about to occur, I had no memory at all.

The blue Renault was there at the corner and in seconds I had reached it. The driver, a thin youth with a beard, was leaning across the front seat with his hand on the open door. 'For God's sake,' he hissed, 'get in. What are you waiting for?'

After long seconds in which everything had happened at a tenth of its normal pace, and every gesture seemed isolated, frozen, time was racing again and my heart with it. I sat slumped over the weapon, shaking so violently now that my teeth chattered. Some part of me was still stranded out there in the lurid square, utterly mesmerized before the kneeling figure of the woman, unable to move. It was a merely physical self that sat sweating in the promised Renault, making at high speed towards a set of traffic lights and very nearly safe on the other side of all this.

So that reality, when it impinged, seemed unreal.

'Oh no,' the driver moaned, swinging violently on to the kerb, 'it can't be! Jesus! Jes-*us*!'

There, immediately ahead, was a roadblock.

He flung open the door and tumbled out, leaving the engine running and the windscreen wipers flicking crazily back and forth, and through the waves of rain I saw lights flashing and uniformed men bearing down upon us. There were shots. At last my own door too was open, and as I stumbled out on to the pavement I thought *Yes, I have seen all this before in the newspapers. In black and white. In the odd, grainy dimension of what is already history*.

I was naked and in the open. Every landmark

beyond the piazza was unfamiliar to me, I was a stranger here and had lost all sense of direction. I hurled myself into an alleyway, hearing the shots die away behind, and felt what must have been the weight of my haversack fall away from me. *Good,* I thought. *So much the lighter. Now I have nothing.* I turned a corner, then another, and found myself in the piazza again – so I did see it a second time – facing the gothic palace with its blind brick loggia. The hearse for the disrupted funeral was there, a great black carriage all agleam in the rain, its glass windows banked with flowers, sable plumes at the corners, before it two coal-black horses solemnly decked and plumed. They lifted their heads as I passed and I caught a flash of white eyeballs. One of them raised a foreleg and struck the pavement, *clang, clang,* with its hoof. I cast myself into the street that curves away to the east of the palace, which had so fascinated me in the photographs and round whose bend in time I had been unable to see. There was no one in sight and no sound of pursuit.

The street with its overhanging eaves continued to curve, with heavy buildings on either side, all their shutters solemnly shut. I began to be breathless, and it occurred to me that with my footsteps echoing as they did between the high walls I might attract less attention if I simply walked.

So I walk.

Out here in the big open square I have come to there has been no rain, not a sign of it. I cross the square, which is deserted, and which seems enormous at the pace I am forcing myself to adopt, turn down a narrow side street and am a little surprised to discover that I am already at the edge of town. There are derelict sheds standing among waist-high thistles, broken fences grown over with old man's beard, stretches of stony ground scattered with rags, paper, plastic bottles, worn car tyres, tennis shoes, rusty food-tins, the gathered wrack and rubbish of existence, and a yard beside a disused cinema where boys have been tinkering with a car. All the parts of it are laid out neatly in the dirt. A blue Renault.

A little further on and I find orchards on both sides of the road, apple trees lit up with late afternoon sunlight and heavy with fruit. I reach up and take one. Bite into it. Eat.

And in the miraculous assurance of being safe at last, walk on under the early blossoms.

EUSTACE

1

The door to the corridor was closed, but a soft light from out there flowed through the tilted fanlight, displaying, in a puzzle of shadow and highlights like a landscape on the moon, the bodies of the sleeping children, some crouched knee to chin in the centre of the bed, some spread-eagled face downward with a footsole extended into the dark, others again laid out straight with their toes to the ceiling, the sheet rucked under their chin and their breath lightly coming and going. There were ten children in the dormitory, all girls. The room was full of their breathing and the faint scent of frangipani from the garden below.

All this, glimpsed from the washroom door, was like something the youth had never seen before.

Even after his eyes had grown accustomed to the half-darkness he found it difficult to interpret details. Was it a pillow one of the children was clasping to her, or another body? Was that a shadow or the dark strands of her hair? Was it an arm or a leg whose rounded flesh the light fell upon and made luminous? Piecing the ten bodies together as his gaze travelled from bed to bed, disentangling shadow from substance, smoothing out the creases in sheets and nightdresses to discover limbs, all this took long minutes in which he simply stood perfectly still and stared.

Then there were the sounds. Locating each of them – the murmured words, the long slow outpourings of breath – and tracking them to an individual child so that he had each of them, each of the ten, clearly in mind; separating out the ticking of a clock, insect-noises from the park, and the dripping – was it? – of a tap in the washroom behind him, or a shower, or a cistern, together with his own breathing and the beating of his blood – it was a task to be carried out methodically and with great patience, but at some lower level than the part of him that simply observed. Something was thinking for him; that is how he might have put it. As when, with a speed and assurance that would have astonished the casual observer, he would lay out, on a sheet of newspaper he could barely read, all the working parts of a machine. Machines were the most complicated things he knew: more complicated than people – though of course he had only himself to judge by – and more reliable as well. Machines he was utterly at home with. Things fitted together part by part according to a settled order, and all the parts were congruent, screw and nut to bolthole, thread to thread. His long fingers could solve any problem of that sort in minutes, no trouble at all. His intelligence was all in his fingertips, and in his eyes.

One of the children began to mutter words out of a dream and the sounds caught his attention. He could

150

make nothing of them. But the idea of a dream breaking into the room like that, the idea of its lying submerged under the silence (which wasn't really silence at all) and breaking surface in those unintelligible syllables, disturbed him; it introduced an unmanageable element. He took a small step forward.

It was a child in the second bed from the end. On the right. Who now turned in her sleep, changing not only her own position but all the highlights and shadows in the room, breaking his grasp of it. The dream had started a ripple that involved all the other sleepers as well. One by one they translated it, more or less according to the depth of their sleep, into stirrings, murmurs, little groans, till the whole room at the level of the beds was a shifting surface of light and dark, of rising and falling contours. He was almost sick with the unsteadiness of it. Everything was out of hand.

He turned back into the dark of the washroom with its row of handbasins and its dripping cistern or shower, sat on the tiled floor and began to haul on his boots, which he had been holding in his right hand, first the one, then the other; carefully knotting the laces. While he was still engaged in this the crack of light on the wall opposite began to widen, a shadow filled it, and when he jerked his head around one of the children was there, standing barefoot in her nightdress, through which he could see the darker outline of the body.

She stood and rubbed her eyes, frowning. She must have been nine or ten years old. She stared and frowned, but didn't seem at all alarmed.

'Hullo,' he said huskily, because he couldn't think of anything else, and because the word, being the ordinary one, seemed immediately right. He gave a nervous smile.

She considered him a moment, then turned away as if he might be merely illusory and went to one of the washbasins.

He got shakily to his feet, suddenly too tall and thin, feeling out of his element in this big empty room with its checkerboard tiles, its row of handbasins and mirrors, its cubicles at the darker end where something dripped. He stood with his back to the door in case she panicked and tried to pass him. She was bent over a basin, drinking from the tap. Then she turned, wiping her mouth with the back of her hand, and considered him again, her brows drawn together in childish puzzlement. He lost his head. 'Look, you won't tell anyone, will you?' he stammered.

She grew thoughtful but said nothing and he began to move towards the window.

'It's a secret,' he said.

She continued to watch. She seemed puzzled rather than afraid.

Fearful that if he took his eyes off her for even a second she might break or cry out, he felt his way to the sill, swung a leg over, eased himself down till only his fingertips clutched the cracked paintwork, and dropped. Once safely on the ground he moved swiftly into the shadow of a tree, but did not move away. Something made him stand there, still in the half-darkness, and look up. The garden trembled all about

152

him on tiny waves of sound that might have been
wings.

The child had come to the sill, her nightdress billow-
ing a little in the breeze. She stood there, quite calmly,
looking down at him. Then she did a strange thing.
She raised her right hand briefly and waved.

2

She told no one.

Waking as usual in the narrow bed, with Miss Ivers
in the doorway briskly clapping her hands and calling
'Now children, now girls!' and the room already filled
with groans, giggles, little shrieks, as the nine others in
their different ways took on the new day, sat dangling
their feet over the edge of the bed a moment, unwilling
to kick off, or wandered about half asleep till the first
water struck them, exuberantly teased, slapped at
sheets and punished pillows, or brushed their hair
with long strokes, counting, or practised whatever
rituals they had need of to make the crossing from the
deep privacies of sleep to this lighter, brighter world
that was embodied in Miss Ivers standing straight and
slim in the doorway, the exclamation mark of her body
making its own clear point: 'This, girls, is how we
should bear ourselves in the face of Monday morning,'

the clapping of her hands, and the 'Now girls', providing the first little hook on which they would hang the many wandering minutes of their day – waking as usual into this utterly orderly disorderly world, she thought she must have dreamed him, the boy in the washroom, he seemed so alien to it all; she put him away with her other dreams as she swung out of bed and drew on her slippers.

But no. In the act of reaching down to ease her finger under the right heel, she saw again the laces drawn tight over his index finger, the freckles on the back of his hand, and knew he was real. Though surrounded still by the soft unreality of her sleep, so that he existed in the continuation of whatever she had been dreaming just before, he had been, none the less, utterly bulky and solid – bare-legged, gangling, freckled, with a smell, a mixture of sweat and car-grease, that did not belong to dreams. Dreams were odourless, she knew that at least. Moving with the others into the washroom she couldn't believe that they too would not catch some trace of his presence, feel some displacement he had made in the ordinariness of the room, with its mirrors above white basins, its shower and toilet cubicles. But the others were washing noisily. They caught no scent of him in their boisterous, not-quite-female world.

He had left no sign.

She told no one, and the day went on as if nothing had occurred. It was organized so tightly, and they moved through it at such a keen pace, that it was difficult to let any new thing in to find a place there:

154

doing mental sums as fast as you could and then sitting up very straight when you had the answer, with your hands on your head and your elbows pushed back – straining, but not too obviously, to be called; vaulting the horse with your chin up and your eyes straight ahead as each of the others, one, two, three, four, went off before you, blonde, black or brown pony-tails swishing; copying, but fast, before the blackboard was turned over, the chief products of Western Australia; all this kept your head filled with so many immediacies that there was no time for day-dreaming, and no corner, with so much that was public and organized, in which anything unusual could lurk. Even when they wrote a composition and had to use their imagination the lines were strictly drawn. Miss Wilson wrote the opening paragraph on the blackboard. It was an old house on Dartmoor, in England, deep in fog, and they went on from there, filling the house with darkness and the sound of creaking doors, that might be ghosts but would more likely turn out to be tramps or stray dogs that left all mysteries explained in a last paragraph, which they were required to label *conclusion*.

Faced with the open invitation to confess a mystery, she might have let the boy in. But he didn't seem to fit. He was too tall, too ungainly, too much part, in his desert boots and T-shirt, of the sprawling subtropical town that began at the walls of their park, to enter the realms of the imagination as Miss Wilson defined it or to find himself on Dartmoor, in England. But she did think of him briefly. She allowed him to approach out

155

of the fog and come up, in his floppy desert boots, to the door of that deserted cottage. Looking vaguely scared, he stood at the threshold, his whole body tense with what might now be required of him. Then she relented and let him off. She let him move away from his meeting with the perfectly conventional spirit she now introduced, who had once, in the olden days, been a witch whom the village people had drowned (though she wasn't really a witch at all, just a crazy old woman) in a greasy millpond, along with her cat called Lock.

There was an occasion during prep. when she considered telling her best friend of the moment, Adele Morgan, who slept in another dormitory; was on the very point of it; but didn't. She had the odd sense that she would not be believed. There was no detail she could produce that would be at all convincing, and she was too matter of fact, had too clear a sense of the real and too high a regard for the truth, to invent one. She would wait till such a detail presented itself.

Besides, she had already anticipated the questions Adele would ask and they were not interesting. 'Did he do anything? Weren't you scared?'

No, he did nothing at all. He was just there. And she hadn't been scared because there was nothing to be scared of. He was just an ordinary boy with red hair. Very tall when he stood up, and very shy. When she first saw him he had been sitting on the floor with one bare knee drawn up so that he could tie his shoelace (one was tied already, the other, drawn taut, was still, after the first simple knot, looped over his forefinger) and she had been reminded of how her younger brother, Jack, had learned to tie laces by practising it over and over, all one morning, on the verandah steps. The boy had had that same look of anxious concentration. It was perhaps his coming to her thus out of her own past that made her believe at first that she was still asleep in her bed and dreaming. That is why she had turned away a moment to look at her cool face in the mirror, to see that her eyes were open, and to drink. When she turned back he had got to his feet and was staring.

A tall boy, carrot-haired and unexplained; but he didn't scare her any more than if she *had* dreamed him. At that odd hour, and in the lingering heaviness of sleep, he seemed like a continuation rather than an interruption of her dreams; as if she had first dreamed him and then found him there. What was there to explain?

Of course his presence wasn't related to her daytime life, to the world of corridors and stairs and stairwells and room where the blackboards were filled, even in darkness, with chalked up facts. But then neither were her dreams. These hours that were for sleep belonged to nowhere. They were outside the rules. No bells governed them, they were free. She had dreamed the strangest things, and had sometimes been very frightened indeed. Once she had dreamed of being on a picnic with her family when a ship rode up the beach that had no sail. The sailors, who were very ragged and foreign-looking, begged for some garment they could rig up to sail home and she had offered her

157

dress, a bright yellow one. They had fixed it to the mast and sailed right out of view on the still moonlight, out of sight of her parents and her two brothers, while she, in one of those strange dreamworld experiences of being quite palpably in two places at once, stood both at the water's edge watching and at the rails of the ship, while the yellow dress (which had not been hers in fact but her cousin Millie's) stood out stiffly in the breeze.

Compared with that, an unexplained but entirely ordinary boy with red hair wasn't extraordinary at all. He had just gulped and said 'Hullo'. But when she stood at the window-sill and watched him, where he was half-hidden below the Chinese elm, he had looked, she thought, like a painting. She saw him in a field struck by the wind, all agitated gold. His long legs, bare, his arms long and hanging at his side, his face tilted towards her, had made him at that moment not 'too tall' as she had first thought but like someone drawn out, drawn upward with the strain of being where he was, or who he was, as in one of the swirly paintings in the school corridor. It was the heightened reality of him that attracted her. As if he belonged to a world with other rules of perspective, or to another order of beings, and had come to induct her into other possibilities than she had so far discovered at home or at school, to reveal to her how she might cross into the further reaches of herself. Until he came into her life she had not known how suffocated she felt here, where every moment of the day was *for* something and had to be filled; or how it frightened her that the whole of life might be like this, that those corridors where you must never run, and stairs you went down only on the left, and *quietly*, might lead to places where the rules that applied were different only in detail, not in kind, and were invisible to her only because no one had ever pointed them out (that was for later, as Miss Ivers said of so many things) or given them names.

So she kept his secret because it was her own, and knew he would come again. She did not even bother to wait for him, since she knew she had only to fall asleep and he would be there; and when he was there she would immediately be awake.

3

Standing again, boots in hand, at the washroom door, he recognized in the scene some benevolence of nature that was reserved only for him. He had not expected it, but there it was. The world often surprised him like this. Behind him the raised window was a funnel for moonlight and the gathered noises of the garden, which he found comforting: soft wing-beats that might be an owl or a flying fox, the shifting of leaves, a stirring of furred creatures hunting. Beyond that, the wall he had come over; which formed in his mind a barrier he had passed between the world outside, that still made itself heard in the distant sound of a car (a Falcon, he guessed, changing gears as it turned uphill), the self they knew from the overalls his mother washed and the underthings she laid out for him, and this other self standing in socks and shorts at the threshold of a different world entirely, a strange still world of children sleeping in rows under bluish sheets, which belonged to the night, to this place only, and was female.

It was to him as if these children slept here always; as if this room were always closed and moonlit, even when it was light elsewhere, because this was the only way he had seen or could imagine it, or cared to. The room hovered above the nightsounds of the garden like a spaceship in a wood, with rows of encapsulated virgins. They slept. They awaited his arrival. The door at the end of the room led nowhere, and the light out there came not from a corridor but from space; nothing familiar lay beyond: no stairways to other parts of the building. This room was its own place, afloat on the children's breathing and on his own will. When he blinked it was not there. It had been waiting – for how long? – till he should at last appear. It was always half-dark and could never be otherwise. Never. Because if he let the light in he would have to let in along with it all those ordinary, exterior events and conditions that belonged to daylight and the sequence of days, which would put it forever beyond him, whereas this way it was entirely his. No past led up to the room and no future away from it. It simply was. And it was here because he had found it here.

He listened to the children's breathing. That too, strange as it might be to him, was a comfort. Its regularity calmed him. Could he find her out, he wondered, by the note of her breath?

He had not seen, on that last occasion, which bed she had come from, but had decided – *he* had decided – that it was from the second bed on the right, in which last time, as he stood here, a body had spoken and stirred. All his re-enactments of that last time, achieved under the pressure of his need to come back here, if only in imagination, had begun with the turning of that body under the sheet, the first mysterious disturbance and coming alive of the still room as he had originally seen it. In his re-living of that moment he had made certain changes; he had allowed himself to see what he had, in fact, only heard. A child rose up out of the second-last bed on the right, met his gaze, swung her legs slowly over into the dark between the beds – he loved this moment, the contact of her bare foot with the cold pavement – and came down between the rows of sleeping forms, her nightdress transparent in the bluish light, holding out her hand to him.

He had been over it so often that he had quite erased that other version in which she surprised him from behind, caught him sitting cloddishly on the floor, struggling with the laces of his boots. In his new version of their meeting he woke her by the force of his own gaze upon her and she came quickly and willingly.

Now he fixed his gaze once more on the second last

bed on the right and waited for her to stir. And was again surprised.

From the first bed on his left came a small gasp; a child pushed herself into a sitting position and their eyes made contact in the dark. She drew down the sheet, swung her legs over. And he thought with a moment's passionate fury that he had been foiled, that the initiative had been stolen from him, and from *his* child, by an impostor. But she did hold out her hand to him, and when she came and stood before him he saw that it was the same child after all.

4

Marylyn Shore had come back to school in the new term with a hamster.

Pets were not allowed, but the hamster had lived for nearly two weeks in a wardrobe in the dormitory. It was Marylyn's, but in sharing the secret of its presence the others had come to think of it as theirs as well. They had fed it biscuits smuggled in from tea, and bits of lettuce and carrot, and were allowed briefly to stroke its fur. It became part of their dormitory life. Their sleep perhaps had a new quality because of their knowledge that it was there at the bottom of the wardrobe, and because, being nocturnal, they knew it was abroad, a tiny heartbeat in the darkness, while they slept. It moved in their sleep. It gave the night a different texture.

But the animal was discovered at last and transferred to the science lab., where Marylyn and the others were still able to feed it but where it passed out of their private world, and the glamorous light of a shared secret, and became just one more of the school's public properties.

Since Marylyn and the rest refused to tell the hamster's name (they had in fact called it Eustace), Miss Wilson, the headmistress, decided on Ruggles.

Because she was so pleased with herself for having found a neat and happy solution to the problem, Miss Wilson made rather a cult of Ruggles; she frequently referred to him in her pep-talks, and pretended, in a way the girls thought childish and affected, that he was a real personage and a full member of what she called 'our raft', so that Ruggles became, in the end, as much one of Miss Wilson's attributes as the motheaten gown she wore, her Eiffel Tower brooch, her green-ink corrections and the tiny bobble of flesh on her left eyelid.

Meanwhile, the creature's shadow, in his incarnation as Eustace, continued to occupy a place in the life of the dormitory, which had substance in a smell they might pick up from the bottom of the wardrobe, or a memory of how his small heart had beaten when they held him, very carefully, between the palms of their hands. Eustace became a code-word. Having left behind his essence, his secret name, the forbidden animal could be evoked out of the darkness of almost any occasion and went on dwelling among them in a form that was invisible to the eyes of the authority and no longer needed feeding with anything but their childish complicity.

It was with the thought of Eustace clearly in mind that Jane decided to keep her visitor entirely to herself. She thought of him now under a code-name, like Eustace, and when he was about to tell his real name once she warned him quickly, 'No, no, you'll spoil it. You mustn't tell your real name. Not to anyone, not even to me.' She knew he would not remain undiscovered forever, that sooner or later the others would certainly find out; but it seemed to her that if she kept her secret name for him, and ·if, for the others, he remained nameless, she would have something at least that was her own and that the boy would be safe.

The others did find out of course, it was inevitable. First Sheryl Payne, then Jill McArthur, then everybody. They sat up in their beds now, except for the sleepiest of them, whenever he came, and watched, and questioned, and tried to steal him away with all sorts of tricks – a different trick in each case, but she always recognized it, she knew them all so well – and with foolish, little-girl stories (how could he be interested in such things?) about their horses, their houses, the places they had been. She had never tried anything like that. It wasn't necessary. It was her bed he sat on; and the others, when gradually over the nights they got used to his presence and had gathered into the familiar atmosphere of the room his odd smell of car-grease – the others, when he had been made safe at last (she at least knew that he was *not* safe) came on tip-toe over the cool floor and sat cross-legged on the beds opposite. From there, gravely, in a little hum of female excitement, they watched. But did not enter the charmed circle. They came only to the edge of it, their faces lit by what they did not understand but felt the glow of just the same, while she and the boy, just the two of them, burned at the centre. There was nothing now, she felt, as she looked out at their scrubbed faces, still a little fuzzy with sleep, that would ever take her back and make her one of them. She had crossed some border in herself that was still, for them, far in the future. There was no way back.

5

The others, watching, saw them as through glass, in a luminous bubble, they were so utterly absorbed in one another, had been drawn into such a distant dimension; and this both fascinated the children and freed them. Accepting the strangeness of the thing, and its attendant glamour, made them spectators and left them untouched.

What they might have been thinking, with a world-liness that was already an aspect of the women they would become, was 'What does she see in him?'. It was a mystery, but the question made it ordinary. What-does-she-see-in-him referred to the boy's patent un-attractiveness, to his being too tall, too red-haired, too freckled, to his having bony knees and bitten-down fingernails that were lined with car-grease. These facts set him in a light so common (as the question itself set the whole situation in the light of 'boyfriends' and 'romance') that they quite forgot the unusualness of his being there at all in the more interesting mystery of his having chosen Jane and of Jane's having chosen him. His ugliness, since it wasn't their affair, seemed endearing. It was only later that they would see these characteristics that had made him safe as part of what also made him monstrous – his grease-stained hands, his being all arms and legs. But by then he would have passed out of the dormitory world, where everything was softened by the hour, the lingering glow of sleep out of which he had woken them, and their own hunger for fairytale, into the panicky blaring of police-sirens and arc-lamps that made the school park with its millions of leaves into a dangerous jungle. Then some of these children, who had sat entranced by the spec-tacle of Jane and her visitor, and had even flirted a little with the unusualness of him, would fly into hysterics; he would rise up out of their sleep, with red hair on the back of his wrists, as a terror they could get around only by crying out aloud, till they found themselves safely awake again in their father's arms.

'This is Eustace,' she had told them on that first occasion. And they stared. Was it a joke? Who would have suspected Jane, dumpy Jane, of having a sense of humour? Or did she mean some sort of transformation? They stared.

Jane concealed a smile at her own cunning. The secret significance of the word, which was already informed with both these possibilities (and was not her name for him) immediately cast its spell, not upon the boy, who remained unchangeable, but on her foolish schoolfellows, for whom he was immediately softened and silvered over and made familiar and small. He slipped into the circle of maidens like a changeling prince; puckering his brow a little, poor boy, and wondering where all this might lead.

She took his hand then, and he relaxed and felt safe. But he thought of the moment later as the point where he first lost control of things, where he was taken over and made an instrument of her more powerful will. What did it mean: Eustace?

But he was delighted at first by these others; by the glow they made in the room, by the increase ten times over of the specifically female atmosphere they created. They were a magnetic field of which he was the centre. Only gradually did it dawn upon him that this wasn't really so. Their attention wasn't a single force, but a set of forces that pulled him many ways. He couldn't keep track of himself. He felt torn apart, felt odd bits of him being passed around from one to the other of these children like sections of an enormous doll, an arm off here, there a leg. They didn't actually touch him, it was something stronger than touching. He felt parcelled out into so many places he no longer knew where his real centre was, if not in the one part of him they seemed unaware of, though he made no attempt to hide it. Their innocence, which had its own wilder aspects, its knot of chaos, had stolen the initiative from him. He became first resentful then cunningly resourceful. These others were a mistake. They wanted to make a pet of him, whereas what he wanted to make of himself was something quite different.

That was his real need here: that the situation should make of him something that he painfully longed for and had come here, all unwitting, to have revealed. He had no idea what it might be. He had simply followed some clue in himself and arrived. He hadn't even suspected, before now, that such a situation might exist, that high up here among the trees there was this room, magically sealed off from the rest of the world, where children slept and awaited his coming. He made no connection between these misty creatures in their nylon gowns and the crocodile of noisy schoolgirls in bottle-green tunics and straw hats that he sometimes passed down at the shops. Wandering about in the dark, blindly, hardly knowing what he was after, driven by his own restlessness, his dissatisfaction with himself and everything about him, simply lunging out into the air, down unfamiliar avenues and side streets, he had come to a wall that suggested climbing, since there must be something on the other side of it, then a garden, then an open window that could be entered, and there it was. It was as if he had climbed into a high place of his own head where he could breathe at last, and confronted it: a situation that had always been there and from which he was to force now the long withheld revelation.

But it had begun to go wrong. He had lost his grip of it.

He wondered sometimes how different things might have been if he had chosen another of the children: the child in the second bed on the right for example. They represented, these nine others, a set of possibilities he had not wakened, dreams or stories he had failed to enter, full vessels stored here unused because he had already chosen, or been chosen by –

So many possibilities confused him. They would have to be removed. He must go back to the beginning and take her with him. To a place where they could make things simple again, just the two of them. To their own place. To the tiled bathroom with its rows of mirrors above handbasins and that slow dripping from one of the cubicles.

6

That was the first step and she made no protest. She too seemed glad to get away. He half-closed the door behind them. It wasn't necessary to close it altogether, that might have alarmed her; and he wouldn't then be able to hear any disturbance from the dormitory. The half-closed door was enough. Here they could be alone, and here he felt the initiative was in his own hands again. He had separated her from whatever there was that she shared with the other children, and which their presence, however supernumerary, might represent. Here in the washroom, with its naked tiles and its own rituals, as of the ordinary public life set aside and the body laid bare, they could rediscover some of the magic that was theirs alone. He could bring his own body into focus here and rediscover what part it was to play in all this. He could see her not as one of a group of maidens, all washed and white in the alien power of their united but generalized sexuality, which if anything set her at a distance from him and disarmed him of his own power, but as herself – soft, real, touchable, as she had been previously only when he summoned up her image during the day, leading her off in his imagination, and being surprised in that dimension how far she was willing to go into his world, how deeply she herself led him on.

So the washroom was the first step.

They took it.

Returning later to the silence of the dormitory, to the hush in which the others almost breathlessly waited, he felt extraordinarily liberated and sure of himself. He would have liked to laugh right out, to throw the door open and shout into whatever lay beyond, or start a pillowfight and see the feathers fly, to do something loud and exuberant and alive with energy; he felt so filled with the joy of things and the power of his own voice and limbs. He would think of this later as perhaps the happiest he had ever been, when between him and the world there had been perfect concord.

If he had given way then to his boyish desire to whoop and break out everything might have been different. But he was thwarted; and not only by his fear of discovery, which in the recklessness of the moment he might have forgotten. The attention of the others, which was focussed entirely on her, had pushed him away to the edge of the scene.

'O Jane, Jane,' their eyes were saying, 'what have you been *doing*?'

She too saw it, and her hand touched his in an attempt to reassure him, but it was too late. He felt a surge of anger, and saw, in the blind fury of it, that he must take her further than the room next door. He must eliminate these others altogether.

So it was that he began to talk of a time when they would run away together. He sulked, he cajoled, he was insistent.

'Will you?' the others asked. Their eyes were hungry for it.

'Yes,' she said firmly. It was as simple as that.

He dared not ask when. All he could do, as the nights mounted up and the pressure grew in him, was to force her closer, till the link between them was stronger than anything that might tie her to the others and their shared existence, till she stood so far beyond their understanding that she no longer had anything to say to them, and the circle in which they glowed when they sat together on her bed in the dormitory dazzled and even burned the gaze; till together they were so far beyond these others that their going would barely be noticed. He thought of their simply rising where they sat, in a kind of air-bubble, and climbing straight up out of sight.

They stood together at the sill, her hand in his, and looked down into the garden. It murmured and was heavy with the scent of night-flowers and the tink-tink of tree-frogs and crickets.

'Will you?' he said. 'Tonight?'

He was, at that moment, the more innocent of the two. The next step, beyond the intimacies of the washroom, appeared to him only in terms that were vague and unimaginable, as some going beyond a point he had not yet glimpsed and therefore dared not press for. Once they were free of the building, down there among the leaves, with earth under his boots and the night all around them, the garden itself would provide the revelation of what it was to be, would speak directly to the blood in his hands. He felt the quickening rhythm of it deep within him.

He had never had a plan. His cunning, such as it was, dealt only with immediate events, and the shape of each occasion as he stepped into it was determined by the elements of the occasion itself and his response to them: a landscape of broken surfaces – light and shadow, cloth and limbs, the black-and-white checkerboard of a bathroom floor, the softness and warmth of her belly under the night-dress, the breathing of leaves under the moon.

'Will you then?' he repeated. 'Tonight?'

She looked down into the pool of nightsounds and saw that to put it off any longer would change nothing, since she had already decided. Another day or two, or twenty. She would have to go beyond this point sooner or later. That had been clear from the start.

'Tonight then,' she said, and heard the long sigh he gave, and felt his slow breath pass her. He was utterly happy. Utterly unaware of what lay before them.

For one last moment they sat together, hand in hand on the sill, and did not move.

7

Later there was to be no reasonable explanation for it. The whole affair would remain, especially to Miss Wilson, for whom they had always been her very own little girls, and models of good behaviour, an impenetrable mystery.

She regarded them now with a kind horror as they copied from the board and embarked on one of her flights of fancy, starting, as always, from the given paragraph: they had fallen, while out walking, into a cave full of brilliant jewels. Marylyn Shore chewed the end of her biro – 'Don't, dear,' she told the child automatically, 'you don't know where it's been.';

Gillian Bell sucked a pigtail, others gazed wide-eyed at the ceiling, or in the case of Bettina Falk, who was left-handed, turned at that odd angle to the desk; each of them already following her own idiosyncratic path, but all just children really, ordinary healthy little girls who would go on from this point (they all hoped) to normal lives. Watching them she felt it as some deficiency in herself that she could not connect them with the children who had sat there night after night with *him*; watching, keeping his secret, allowing Jane –

She felt a little jump of panic at letting Jane back here among the others, as if she might bring into the room, poor child, some of the terrible knowledge she must have acquired *out there*.

Miss Wilson put her hand over her mouth, not to cry out, it was too awful. It threatened to send the whole afternoon flying in splinters. She had to hang on.

But how could they have permitted it? She simply could not comprehend. Allowing Jane to go off like that, without a word of protest, without the least signal of alarm. And even worse perhaps, since it wasn't a single occasion but a matter of days – no, weeks – sitting night after night watching the boy, and even, since they were impenetrably united these children, inveterately secretive, touching him, allowing him to touch them . . .

At first they had refused to speak at all, they simply shook their heads and were dumb; even when, as gently as possible, they had been made to *understand*; when the awful facts were made clear to them – or as clear as was necessary: what had happened to Jane, and how close they themselves had been to ultimate harm. Even then they revealed no details, they refused to speak out. Had they failed to comprehend the horror of it? Or were they merely stubborn in the defence of their own complicity, or unfeeling, or – yes that, surely – protecting themselves from the full knowledge of what they knew. They had simply gone on, in a way that alarmed and affronted her, as if nothing had occurred at all.

They were writing now with their heads bent to the task, filling the first page with the fruits of their imagination. Later she would read what they had written and give it a mark. She comforted herself with the thought that if their imagination stopped at a certain point it was just as well. It would save them, as she could no longer save herself, from the enormity of the thing.

She glanced quickly at her watch. 'Time, children,' she said briskly. 'You have two more minutes. Make sure you have a concluding paragraph, label it, and see that your name is printed clearly at the top of the page.'

She stood at the window, with her arms clasped to her breast as if she were cold, though it was in fact too warm today. The garden below was approaching the full thickness of summer, every leaf separate and astir in the afternoon breeze, discovering darkness as an edge of shadow, the hungry little birds dipping and feeding on berries and squabbling disgracefully over the remains.

And in one way or another they had accepted it, the others. They allowed Jane, who had never been popular among them, and whose face soon grew dim in their minds, to walk out of their lives as she had walked out of the dormitory and made as little as possible of her failure to come back.

The event itself remained for them a series of glowing but unreal moments when they had sat on a bed in the unlighted dormitory and watched Jane and the boy, two figures already touched by the strangeness of distance and the night; high dreamlike occasions between stretches of sleep, when they had, briefly, touched on something outside the rules of their daily existence, the rules that would govern their lives afterwards, and which they knew now was *there*, had always been there, and would never, even in their own case, and despite the rules, be entirely exorcised; though it did not have to be confronted – or not yet. They would recognize it again later, at a point further on, past the husbands and the children still to come. It was ten years off for one, at the bottom of twelve feet of water; twenty years for another, for others fifty, sixty even. It would reappear in a different and quite unpredictable form to each one of them: as a tree trunk suddenly illuminated on a country road, every scribble in its bark clearly readable; or a lump secretly nourished in one of the soft parts of the body; or a welling up, beyond the faces of children and grandchildren, of a sea of blood. At that moment they might understand her at last, their lost schoolfellow, and in whatever part of themselves they harboured a memory of all this, without precisely recalling it, see themselves getting up out of their solid childlike bodies to follow.

Meanwhile there was Miss Wilson's essay to finish –
the marvellous cavern to be got out of.

They wrote on.

THE PROWLER

1

There is more goes on in this suburb than meets the eye. But naturally.

Waiting at McAllister's newsagency yesterday for a magazine order I overheard a conversation between our popular newsagent and Doctor Cooper of Lancaster Road. 'You know, McAllister,' the doctor remarked, 'you must be about the most regular man, time-wise, in this whole city. I hear your wagon turn into Arran Avenue in the morning and I say to myself, "That's McAllister. It must be five-thirty. Time to get back into my clothes and go home." ' McAllister was delighted. Three minutes later he was repeating the story to a new customer as an example of the complete reliability of his service.

There's no better place than a newsagent's for finding out what goes on in the world. And I don't mean by reading the papers.

2

Ours is one of the older suburbs, no longer fashionable as it was forty or fifty years ago but still retaining a certain desirable elegance, and still, with its expansive gardens and tree-lined avenues, a place where a mode of life can be observed that has not yet surrendered to the patios, clothes-hoists and drive-in supermarkets of the Estates. Houses here are of painted weatherboard in the colonial style: with gables, turrets, pepperpot domes, bull's-eye windows of emblazoned glass, verandahs, wrought-iron railings and venetians that hum in a storm. Bougainvillea and Cardinal Creeper grow thick over outhouse roofs and the lattice-work that keeps out the westering sun. Lawns planted with old-fashioned natives like hoop-pine and bunya, along with the deodars and Douglas firs of empire, make secluded spaces, some of them close to parklike, where willy-wagtails feed and fat grasshoppers wobble in flight above the cannas. It's a quiet area. Lawn sprinklers weave elaborate loops and figures-of-eight; kids on bicycles hiss over the gravel; a station-wagon driven by a young housewife rolls along under the bouhineas, delivering a kindergarten group or a riot of small footballers. Deep in a garden somewhere, a splash, then laughter as children lark about in a backyard pool. That's the nearest you might come to a disturbance of the heavy stillness. At night a tennis court, one wire wall thick with cestrum, suddenly lights up in the sub-tropical dusk and there will be, for an hour or two, the leisurely *thwack thwack* of a ball.

So that the assaults, when they broke out, seemed especially shocking.

3

The earliest victims were disbelieved. They were written off as hysterical. Two of them were unmarried, one was a young mother of three with a history of mental illness, another a schoolgirl of sixteen. It was only after the sixth or seventh attack that one of the newspapers got on to the story, and almost overnight, it seemed, we had a prowler. From that point on, the assaults ceased to be imaginary.

Scarcely a day has passed since then without a new report. Once the prowler entered our lives, via the columns of the paper, he was everywhere. He dominated the headlines and became the obsessive subject of even the most casual conversations. He began, little by little, to change the fabric of our lives. So local school-girls no longer walk up from the bus-stop alone. They ring from town and are met by anxious fathers in the Holden Kingswood. Wives, returning home from a meeting, have learned to drive with the doors locked and the windows up, waiting in the garage till some-one appears on a lighted verandah to see them safely inside. What did we do with ourselves before there was the prowler? What did we talk about? He is as much part of our lives now as the milkman or the newsagent. Every suburb has its prowler and we have ours. It is, the newspapers tell us, the price we pay for modern living. Prowlers come to us as part of that 'way of life' that elsewhere in the papers we are urged at all times to defend.

4

Not all of the attacks follow the same pattern.

Sometimes the prowler does no more than watch a sleeping woman from the window-sill or from the foot of the bed. When she starts awake at last, suddenly aware of a real presence in her dreams, he signals with his forefinger to his lips that she should not cry out, shows the edge of a knife, and then just sits, holding her thus – captive, mesmerized – till the light begins to grow in the room and his face, a darkened blank against the sky, is in danger of becoming clear. Then, without a word, he rolls over the sill and is gone.

Often, while the woman is washing up at the sink, he slips in behind out of the darkening house; an arm goes round her waist, a hand covers her mouth, she feels his breath, his fingers, but sees nothing. On some of these occasions, startled by the sound of a step on the verandah, or a train whistle, the attacker will break and run, and the last she will hear of him is the banging of a wirescreen door – which from that moment onwards will always mean 'assault'. Sometimes the man is naked. More often he is not. There are times when he has been sighted by a curious neighbour, but only rarely are these sightings reported till after the event. One wonders why. What, standing there at the bathroom window or behind the slats of the venetians, did the observer make of a naked figure stalking across the lawn? What area of a neighbour's secret life did he think he had stumbled on, that might be observed but not violated? There are lines, it seems, that we are conditioned not to cross. Does the prowler know this, and feel certain that in nine cases out of ten, even if sighted, he will not be betrayed? His assurance comes perhaps from the very fact that he is a prowler: that is, one for whom the lines exist to be crossed.

5

Under pressure of public opinion, and after a series of heavy editorials, the Police Department has decided to set up a special section to deal with the assaults. Called the Incident Squad, it is under the direction of Senior Detective William Pierce, who has two full-time assistants. One of them, following on a petition to the Department from local women's groups, is a woman.

Senior Inspector Pierce is a widower, aged thirty-nine, with two small boys.

6

It might be anyone.

A fresh-faced kid running round an oval after dark stands panting for a bit with his hands on his hips, then dips his head like a big wading-bird to ease the muscles of his neck. After a brief burst of running on the spot, he resumed his training, alternating stretches of steady jogging with fifty-metre sprints, a lone figure on the darkening oval, a speck of white, moving fast, moving slower, moving fast again against a field of green. Minutes later he is dropping on all fours under a lighted window.

To watch.

At last, slipping out of his gym-shoes, unzipping his track-suit, easing the elastic of his shorts, he stands for a moment in the summer dark – still, poised as if before a barrier he must clear, preparing himself inwardly for the effort it will take, raising himself lightly on the balls of his feet. Then he moves.

Or a man rolls to one side of the bed where his wife is turned heavily away and sets his footsoles on the floor; pushes himself upright, slowly, lest the bed creak; stands, creeps to the hallway. Having learned the cat-like quietness of his movements, and also perhaps his need for violence, in this very house and from the woman he leaves dreaming in the bed behind him. He pauses outside the room where his children sleep and listens a moment to their breathing. Then goes on.

It might be either of these.

Or a painter's apprentice already naked under his white overalls (who sets his lunch-tin down very carefully beside a garden tap) or a grease monkey naked under his blue ones.

Or a man in shorts and singlet, slap-footed in thongs, who has been walking a muzzled greyhound. He ties it now to a tree, flicks his lighted butt into a camellia bush, and smiling, eases up a window. Already in his imagination he is halfway in. Behind him the dog stands tense, quivering, then as the garden sounds grow familiar settles to wait.

It might be any of these.

It might be anyone.

7

The Incident Squad had issued an identikit picture, assembled from the evidence of nearly seventy victims.

Each victim is presented with the outline of a face and a booklet containing page by page a variety of features; as for example, eyes close set or far apart, small pig-eyes, gimlet slits, round eyes frank and open, eyes that bulge a little, eyes that slant upwards at the corner, eyes that slant down, eyes with heavy lids, flat lids, no lids at all; eyebrows far apart or joined at the bridge of the nose, arched, pointed, straight, tilted up or down; eyebrows thick, thin, tufted etc.; and so on for the various shapes of nose, mouth, chin, ears, the various colours and kinds of hair. When each of these features has been considered, and the chosen eyes, eyebrows, nose, mouth, hair, affixed to the plastic outline, a face takes shape and the prowler begins slowly to emerge out of the victim's memory, out of the fog at the back of her head. Feature by feature he comes into focus; and so vividly in some cases that the victim has immediately gone into shock at conjuring up, once more, the image of her assailant.

So then: seventy men recreated out of the dark experience of seventy different women. These seventy images are then superimposed one upon the other to discover what is common to them.

The results are puzzling.

Three separate types emerge, and have now been promulgated as possible likenesses of the prowler.

Three? Can the prowler then change his form? Is he perhaps an expert at disguising himself?

For the fact is that some of the features the women are most insistent upon – as for example black hair closely cropped and a zapata moustache – cannot be reconciled with others, long blond hair like a surfie's, thin pale beard etc. The various images have been further sorted and amalgamated, and so we have the prowler's three faces, one young, one middle-aged, one old, rather like that mysterious portrait attributed to Titian in which the three heads of youth, maturity and old age rise from a single trunk and look in three different directions – a whole lifespan, as it were, telescoped into the space of a single frame. In Titian's case the triple portrait has a pendant, a reflection, in which the three human heads are replaced by those of animals: lion, fox and dog.

But to return to the identikit pictures. What seems strangest is that when the sharply detailed memories

189

of these women have been laid one over the other to produce a composite picture, the face that emerges is both immediately recognizable (because typical) and at the same time quite useless as a key to identification. The three faces are clichés. They look like everyone and no-one. Blondish baby-faced youth, lean, shy-looking, with the beginnings of a moustache – student, bank clerk, apprentice plumber, railway porter. Clean-cut young married with short back and sides – an architect perhaps, or a schoolteacher or swimming-pool contractor, someone in advertising or the Town Clerk's office. Older man, distinguished-looking but with a hint of looseness about the mouth; might be a travelling salesman, a greenkeeper, or a professional soldier recently cashiered or the owner of a small grocery business.

But these images will get us nowhere. Half the male population of the suburb, of the city even, might move without difficulty into these familiar outlines.

What does it mean?

Are there, quite simply, three prowlers of different ages? Or are the women's memories in some way inaccurate – or not so much inaccurate as so creative, so deeply stimulated, that they have added to their experience and remade it, so that what they reproduce is not what they saw at the moment of the attack (some of them can have seen very little) but what sprang into their minds as a visual equivalent of what their hands encountered in darkness, rough cloth, metal, the coarseness of hair, of what forced itself into their nostrils as an unforgettable but unidentifiable odour, and into their ears as a series of obscene monosyllables or grunts or beery endearments. These details do not interest the police; they can do nothing with them.

'His breath on my neck' – what use is that?

'His body was so hot – like an oven.'

'There was a smell of mice.'

'Salt. His hand tasted of salt.'

The visual features of the identity-kit picture are attempts to render, in another language, what the women did not see but sensed, or heard, or smelled, and the translations are clichés, they derive from the common pool of their reading or from the movies. What the identikit pictures provide us with is not the composite picture of a prowler – some citizen engaged at this moment in delivering bread or sealing envelopes in an office or teaching his kids to box with a bag under the house – but a picture of the man these women fear most, or know best, or most long for, or have dreamed of once on some remote occasion and forgotten.

It is no coincidence that if we treat these pictures as caricatures, the man who most resembles the victim's assailant is often a member of her own family: a father, an uncle, a brother-in-law, a son.

8

A burglary takes place. Nothing much is stolen. But a man, turning afterwards to the drawer where his handkerchiefs are kept, discovers that one of them has been used. He stares at the patch of quite ordinary wetness and feels panic. Not disgust but panic. As if his house could never be his own again; as if it stood roofless and could never again offer him refuge or protection because there is no such thing in the world; as if he himself stood naked. Whimpering with shame he tumbles the handkerchiefs out on to the floor and removes them with a stick.

What unnerves him is not the patch of wetness itself, but what it forces upon him – the fact of the burglar's ordinariness and at the same time his utter strangeness. He has before him the man's bodily juices, but no face, no name, and it comes home to him that he lives among strangers, more than half a million of them, who might at any moment break the un-written contract and force their way into his bedroom, open his tallboy, put to use one of his initialled hand-kerchiefs.

Later he comes to think of his reaction as excessive and finds it difficult to isolate the precise cause of his panic. It seems irrational. But it is precisely this irrationality that continues to exert an influence on him. When he thinks of the incident he burns with shame.

So it is that many of the attacks – perhaps even the majority – go unreported.

9

Each morning nearly a dozen women appear at the office of the Incidents Squad with information they will impart only to Senior Detective Pierce in person.

Senior Detective Pierce has become a popular figure in our little world. Smilingly reassuring when he appears on television, grim and determined when he is snapped at press conferences, he is a sort of prowler in reverse who has caught the imagination of the public in much the same way as the prowler himself. What did we do, we ask ourselves, before we had Senior Detective Pierce?

Even the genial detective's two small boys have entered the pantheon. They are called Sam and Harry, aged ten and seven.

They bear no clear resemblance to Senior Detective Pierce but are said to be the living picture of his dead wife, whose absence lends a touch of pathos to the policeman's rugged assurance and brings to an image that is otherwise all assertiveness and power an engaging ambiguity. It allows him to be a family man, very solid and reliable, but also turns him loose.

The two boys, tough-looking blonds, keep the mother's figure clearly in view (did she really look like that?) but in their cocky imitation maleness it is disturbingly redefined. When Senior Detective Pierce and his boys are photographed together at a swimming carnival or at one of our local rugby matches, this simultaneous absence and presence of the wife and mother constitutes a mystery that women respond to (and some men as well) without at all knowing what is in play. Around the rough edges of the two boys, all grazed elbows and knees, glows the aura of the missing wife, and the hard outline of Senior Detective Pierce, ex-lifesaver and Leagues forward, is softened as he stoops to see that Sam's windcheater is buttoned, or with the corner of a handkerchief wet with spit, cleans ice-cream from Harry's shirtfront, by the lineaments of the tender, all solicitous mother.

'How are Samnharry?' women tend to enquire as a way of easing themselves into their story, slipping thus, as they might see it, into the role of family friend or next-door neighbour.

Then immediately, breathlessly, before the proud father can answer: 'I have *seen the prowler!*'

10

The information provided by many of the victims has no basis in fact. That is quite clear. But it is not therefore false. They *have* seen the prowler, but in one of those dreams that nightly crowd the streets of our suburb with a life as intense, as busy, as any it knows by day. Here is just one of them.

The dreamer is a woman of forty, a pharmacist. She is walking at dusk along the grassy footpath of a street planted with poincianas, so thick (it is early summer) that they meet above the roadway, making a tunnel that the light of the street lamps barely penetrates. In the woman's dream the darkness in which she is walking is thickened by an unseasonable fog. It swirls so densely about her that she cannot see her feet. She wades in it. (This is dream weather. No such conditions occur in our damp sub-tropical city at the hour at which the woman is walking; though they are not infrequent, in another part of the year, in the hour before dawn – that is, at the time of her dream.) It is in a state of great weariness, as she drags her body through the warm fog, that she hears behind her, or in front, for she cannot tell which, a soft thudding, the footsteps as she quickly perceives of an approaching jogger.

She stops, flattens herself against the trunk of a tree; hoping that the runner, whoever he may be, will not see her.

The footsteps get closer.

She presses her body closer to the tree-trunk, trying to pass through the rough bark into it, to become part of its life, and seems for a moment to have succeeded. She is not there. Only the roughness of the bark, its pressure round her thighs, gives her some sense of her own separate being as the runner (it is the blond boy in the tracksuit we have previously imagined) materializes out of the fog.

And at that moment a woman she recognizes, with horror, as her perfect double steps right into his path. The runner has to pull up with a jerk to avoid colliding with her. They stand face to face. The youth steps to the left in order to pass her, and her reflection steps to the right. Again they are face to face. She tries to scream but cannot, her voice belongs to the double. She wakes with her face contorted in a silent shriek, and the boy's features are so clearly before her that she can describe them in detail: colour of eyes blue; a scar under the right eye high up on the cheekbone, which gives him a slight squint; hair heavy with sweat, hanging in bangs over his brow; a day's growth of stubble; a film of spittle that makes his teeth gleam, when recovering his breath at last, he opens his mouth to defend himself. She shakes her head. No! No! No defence! No defence possible!

196

It is the boy in the tracksuit, no doubt of it. She gives his picture to the life. For a whole week, each night of fog, he pads softly through her sleep and confronts her, always at the same point; comes so close she can smell his sweat, feel his breath on her face. He is too breathless to speak and she too terrified to cry out. They do their strange dance on the grass in utter silence.

After the seventh night of this silent intimidation she goes to the police. The boy enters their files. He contributes his features to one of the three identikit pictures, but is never sighted.

11

It is easy of course to get things out of proportion, to forget that on a night when one, maybe two attacks take place, hundreds of innocent girls sit at their dressing-table mirrors with the window open, rubbing coldcream into their face and neck, smoothing it gently upwards, then lower themselves into untroubled sleep; that schoolboys, tired after late football practice and an hour of television, roll gently over the touchline into absolute oblivion before they have even resolved the question, with fingers round their cock: 'Will I tonight or won't I? Did I do it last night?'; that young lovers in cars angle-parked towards the drop on Bartley's Hill are softly rediscovering one another, moving into a lifetime together as they uncover the familiar unfamiliarity of one another's bodies in the hot darkness; as their parents, in a space of dark between the streetlights below, are also moving through one another (having graduated from here more than twenty years ago) like palpable ghosts, towards the mystery of sleep and the odd messages, important, uncatchable, that come to them in flashes before dawn.

The suburb sleeps. Most of its dreams are dull, bursting like bubbles in the light, and as clear as bubbles. Entirely guiltless. The sleepers drift, go under, climbing back into the shallows every hour in phase after phase, feeding on stillness; pulse slow, breath regular, renewing themselves with huge draughts of space in which there are no objects to catch the eye or engage the body's idling senses; free for a time of the body's demands as it goes its own way through the dark. Cats are abroad. Their eyes redden under a culvert. Flying foxes row in to raid a patch of Moreton Bay figs at the edge of a golf course or a backyard mango-tree; they hang there, upside down under the boughs, like the souls of a suburb of sleepers, ranked in the dark. Just before first light the newsagent, McAllister, from a car with one whole side cut away, tosses the morning papers rolled into a cylinder on to dew-damp lawns, and Dr Cooper, hearing him turn into Arran Avenue, will know that it is time to get back into his clothes and go home. The papers lie there in the growing light. They carry the news. But the night's real occurrences will not be in them. One or two extraordinary moments, yes: a car-smash on Ipswich Road, a fight in a roadside café on Petrie Terrace, another assault. But not the familiar couplings, the exchanges, the busy life the suburb pursues in its sleep. This is anti-news, and from this point of view the papers are unreliable. Too much that happens here is of no interest to them. *A hundred and fifty thousand potential victims un-attacked in a single night*. What sort of news is that?

12

The CIB has just announced that according to their experts the Nundah prowler and our prowler, who were thought to be one and the same, are indisputably different.

How, one wonders, do they know?

Nundah is the next suburb from here, the boundaries being the suburban railway line, a park, and the winding course of a creek that is quite visible in old photographs of the area but has long since been filled in to make an equally winding street; both sides of the street are planted with bouhinia, which all flower in the same exuberant pink and at the same season, but one side is Nundah and the other is not.

Does the Nundah prowler never cross the street? And if not why not?

I can understand that he might hesitate at the railway-line, which does after all represent a real obstacle and where the character of the two suburbs is distinct, our side being older and better established, with big parklike gardens and, as the real-estate agents put it, a better class of resident. One can imagine that the Nundah prowler, used to small houses on sixteen-perch allotments, mostly treeless and unsewered, might feel intimidated before the big verandahed mansions on our side, might find the gardens, with their clumps of dark shrubbery and shade-trees, off-putting in some way, being unused to their odd pattern of moonlight and shadow or the sound of creatures rustling and breathing in the boughs. Insufficiently urbanized is what he might find them, and threatening to his sense of space. And the same would be true of the old-fashioned interiors. Too many rooms, too many corridors and stairways. Or it might be the unfamiliarity of the life that is lived here that makes him insecure. Or the kind of woman. One understands well enough that there may be social frontiers, and with them a whole set of sexual associations, that a prowler is unwilling to cross. At the railway-line anyway.

But what about further down, where the boundary between the two suburbs is little more than a bureaucratic convenience? Does the Nundah prowler really stick to one side of the street, leaving the other to our prowler? Is some sort of territorial instinct in operation? Do prowlers lay down a scent that keeps off rivals, creating a magic fence around the borders of their fantasy world that a stranger recognizes and is repelled by or finds himself unable to penetrate? And if this is so, how extraordinary that these private boundaries should follow exactly the line laid down on a map in the Surveyor's Office and recognized by most citizens only when their water rates arrive in a different post from their neighbour's opposite – should follow, that is, all the twists and turns of an underground creek filled in nearly sixty years ago and chosen then, quite arbitrarily (we can imagine the debate that was to determine so much in the lives of future prowlers and their victims) as a surburban dividing-line by a committee of respectable aldermen.

No doubt these considerations have occurred to the Incident Squad and been properly dealt with. But they have not published their reasons. When they do so a great deal may be revealed that at the moment remains inexplicable, and valuable light shed on the secret life of suburbs – not to mention the anthropology of prowlers.

13

Despite the warnings that are published almost daily in our papers, and the growing number of assaults, women continue to make themselves vulnerable.

Driving slowly round the suburb in the gathering dusk I see window after window in the dark gardens ablaze with light, open to the cool summer breeze and all the scents, subtropical, overpowering, of the night: jasmine, honeysuckle, cestrum – that heavy night-walker.

The scenes that appear in these brightly lit squares constitute a series of frames between spaces of dark, a living peepshow. Here a girl in a half-slip is ironing, her thin shoulders moving to the music behind her, which as I drive on, bounces a moment and is gone. Another woman at a kitchen bench is decorating a birthday cake in the shape of an open book; my kids will be at the party where it is to be eaten, among party-hats, whistles, bowls of jelly and ice-cream (two dozen moulds of raspberry jelly are cooling on the laminex bench) and off-key renderings of *For He's a*

Jolly Good Fellow. Yet another woman stands in half-thought at a washing machine, holding an armful of overalls and waiting for the cycle to begin.

They are all unaware, these women, in their ease of movement or in their dreamy repose, that they are not only clearly visible as they hang aloft there in the dark, but have been endowed, in their detachment within the single frame, with a special quality of significance, so that the smallest of their gestures strikes the senses, is incised on the memory, is given, in all its ordinariness, an aura of the exotic that suggests a pose, as if what we were really watching were a set of professionals acting out a series of domestic scenes in such a way as to emphasize what is specifically erotic in them.

Even later, towards midnight, when the bluish-silver of the television screens has drained away down a pinhole and the suburb sleeps – all its citizens still present but communally engaged now in reassembling the facts of their daily life into the other language of dreams – even then, I notice, there are casements ajar, obliquely taking the moonlight, a curtain's drift and fall shows where a sash window has been raised a little to let in the breeze.

Not me is what is being proclaimed. *Others may fall victim, but not me.*

Some of these windows are open invitations. But which? That is the point. Obviously the prowler cannot judge or his attacks would not be reported. Do the reported attacks, then, represent only the tip of an iceberg, the prowler's *errors*, his misreading of what a window left unlatched or a woman moving half-clad across a stage-lit space might innocently suggest? Are there rooms where women wait night after night for the sound of a footfall, the creak of a board on the verandah, or a doorhandle being tried, only to suffer, night after night, the entry of nothing more than moonlight, thin, disembodied, that in the morning leaves no mark on the flesh?

The signs are not clear enough. What we need is a more specific means of communication. If only so that some women may discover the signals they should avoid.

14

I wonder, since so much of the objective evidence has led nowhere, if the Incident Squad shouldn't try something quite different; as a way, I mean, of releasing the crimes for a moment from the world of fact into the world of fantasy where they properly belong. Since fantasy and its irrational associations are the language the prowler speaks, mightn't we try thinking in that language as a way of anticipating his moves? At the very least the sort of games I am proposing would loosen things up, get rid of preconceptions that may be standing in the investigators' way, would send them back to the evidence with a more open and intuitive understanding of that pattern of analogies that lies often enough under the confusions of mere event. Several 'Letters to the Editor' have suggested the employment of a clairvoyant. But this is so much simpler. And there is something liberating in the very idea of a group of policemen and women, under the direction of Senior Detective Pierce, abandoning their files for a morning to play party-games.

So then, a questionnaire:

What colour does the prowler bring to your mind?
Apple green.
What fish?
A squid.
What great novel?
Elective Affinities.
What pop record?
Dark Side of the Moon.
What flower?
Datura.
What cloud formation?
Cumulus.
What animal?
Puma
Could the prowler be a Gemini?

When they had learned to enter into the spirit of the thing, and felt properly confident, the investigators would apply this method of questioning to some of the victims. It would be interesting, anyway, to see what might emerge.

15

There are those of us, I think, for whom the final identification of the prowler would be a terrible disappointment. He has become a kind of hero. Jokes that used to be told about a commercial traveller or the milkman invariably begin these days: 'Have you heard the one about the prowler?' Not only is he endowed with a quite fabulous member and a back, as one of our great writers once put it, 'to encounter a hundred in a night', he also, it seems, has a social sense (he is the Robin Hood of the boudoir) and a sense of humour. 'I hope the prowler gets you!' a four-year-old hisses at his mother, who has denied him a second slice of chocolate cake in a department-store café. Bogey man, outlaw, sexual athlete, violator of middle-class security, hero of Husband's Lib – who could possibly want to see all this reduced to the inevitably smaller and commoner dimensions of the truth?

Besides, if the man were identified at last as the one and only prowler, his crimes too would be identified – the real ones – and the rest would be revealed as fantasy, crimes of the mind. Rumours would immediately fly about that he wasn't the real prowler at all but a scapegoat, and that the real prowler was still loose. Women would refuse to recognize him. 'No. *My* attacker was quite different. Taller. More brutal looking. It's not him at all.' The police would be accused of a cover-up of their own inefficiency. And sure enough, the attacks would immediately resume. If the prowler ceased to exist we would have to re-invent him. Perhaps he has already been re-invented several times over.

The police, of course, are well aware of the difficulty. They have to catch the prowler but also to put a stop to the assaults. The first is still a possibility, the second is not. 'You can arrest a prowler, but how do you arrest an epidemic?'

This little joke is attributed to Senior Detective Pierce; who also, it seems, has a sense of humour.

16

And what are his thoughts, the prowler, when eavesdropping in the supermarket on the endless speculations about his identity, or consulting the headlines in McAllister's newsagency to discover where it was precisely, in the maze of suburban streets, that he made his appearance the night before, wait – perhaps for the newspaper to confirm that he was there after all and to provide details he failed to collect in the confusion of the event itself, the woman's age, whether or not she was married, the number of her children – what does he think when, searching the pages for a full account (for public interest has waned, he has been relegated to page seven) he finds that assaults he never committed are now being attributed to him and others that he did commit have been distorted out of all recognition, either by the woman's account of his activities or the newspaper's reporting of them? Has he begun to realize that the real acts have long since been stolen from him, that events to which he brought his whole body and a lifetime of passionate fantasy have passed out of his hands into the public imagination and been stripped there of all the details that made them significant (for the attraction of the ritual lay in a secret order that made no sense to others), decked out instead with journalistic clichés and given a spurious shape that reflects only the moralism of our newspapers, their preference for the monstrous, and their dependence on the rhetoric of romantic novels, television serials and softcore pornography? He has become a victim of the newspaper's hunger for events, but only for those events it has already created in its own dream-factory. How could he ever break through and make them report one of his crimes as he sees it, as it really is? Meanwhile he feels used, manipulated. In his passage across strange gardens, through strange rooms and the bodies of unnamed women, he is no longer pursuing his own will, or even his own fantasies, but acting out a scenario whose lines have already been determined by the newspaper and its readers and will be fully revealed to him, the actor, only in the dirty black-and-white of a few paragraphs of print.

Does he long now to be caught at last, our outlaw, and released from the burden of other men's compulsions, other men's dreams?

The CIB has decided to take further measures. The Incident Squad, retitled the Special Assaults Section, is to be increased from three to seven and will have access to a computer.

Of course bureaucracy tends to increase quite independently of demand, but this new move does seem to be justified. The number of assaults has reached triple figures.

Budgetary considerations, the Minister announces, will allow for a second expansion at the end of the financial year, 'should eventualities require it.' And of course they will.

18

Now that the number of victims has reached the magic figure of a century there are seven identikit pictures, and the strange thing is that they are no longer the clichés of three months ago; each of them has now developed a distinctive character. What we are faced with, it seems, is seven prowlers, all working in the same strictly defined area and using the same methods.

This surely is too much of a coincidence. The work of the prowler begins to look like the cooperative efforts of a gang; except of course that by their very nature these crimes are private and solitary. Or perhaps a club has been formed to act out the attacks as they have been described in the newspaper. A bizarre notion! Who would devise such an entertainment and why? Still, imitators there are, and more than one of them. Of this the police have no doubt.

And how does the prowler himself feel about this, the original prowler, I mean, the initiator, whose integrity consists in his commitment to his own crimes? How strange if his path should cross that of one of the others, if they should meet face to face over the body of a victim; or stranger still, if two of the false prowlers should meet, each just sufficiently like the original to be recognizable but each seeing in the other enough that is different to make clear how much of themselves they have allowed to creep in, to what an extent they are no longer imitators of the prowler but significant variants. If two of the false prowlers were captured would there be enough in common between them for the real prowler to be identified? And supposing all seven to be taken, would it be clear which of them was real? All seven, as the police know, would lay claim to the first attack, might even create a prior one, in order not to be deprived of the rest. (Perhaps one might guess that the least insistent of them, assured of his authenticity, would be the true original.) This is clear from the large number of men who have already come forward and confessed to the crimes. Men of all ages and occupations, from a fifteen-year-old schoolboy to a retired ship-builder of seventy-seven: widowers, pensioners, young men newly married, metho-drinkers, known homosexuals – all desperate, it would seem, to have the prowler's acts define them.

Some of these men simply want to draw attention to themselves. Others have become obsessed with the assaults and long to be their perpetrator, to appropriate to themselves the daring, the fierce aura of sexuality they believe the prowler must be possessed of, his deep sense of relief when, returning to his own house, he stands naked before the mirror and says 'Yes, I am the prowler', or, concealing his violence behind a front of patient domesticity, slips in quietly beside his wife.

There are those among these men who genuinely believe they are the prowler. Faced under the glare of the arc-lamps with indisputable proof that they are not, they break down and sob, they plead with Senior Detective Pierce to examine the evidence again, to find something, some small detail, that will convict them; they resist, they fight, they clutch at straws. Senior Detective Pierce finds these men pathetic. Of all the males in the suburb, they alone are above suspicion, since the one thing they lack (what else does their behaviour mean?) is the courage to commit the crime.

As for the others, the self-confessed prowlers who know they are lying, Senior Detective Pierce has begun to dread their arrival, more even than a new victim. Each of them has a bad conscience. Confessing to the prowler's crimes is a kind of diversion tactic. It is meant to save them from confessing to the real crime they have committed – or think they have committed. They are men who are laden with guilt, who hope that punishment and conviction for one crime, even if it is not their own, will be sufficient and will relieve them of dread. The real crime, in some cases, is trivial, the anxiety is not. And it is the weight of all this secret guilt that Senior Detective Pierce finds so oppressive, since he cannot absolve the men of it, and could not, even if he were to extend to them the one thing in his dispensation, the recognition that the prowler's crimes are theirs. Faces with the men's despair when he declares them innocent, their deep sense of grievance, their sullen hostility, Senior Detective Pierce, on one or two occasions, has come close to breaking down. He has been trained to deal with crime – specific incidents – not with deep, unspecified guilt.

Still, information about all these men is fed into the computer; they become part of Senior Detective Pierce's memory bank. Even if they did not commit the prowler's crimes they reflect them. Only when all the facts have been collated, and many things that are not facts as well, will some sort of pattern emerge.

But when will that be? And what pattern?

Senior Detective Pierce has come to believe, as the

212

number of victims continues to rise and the identikit pictures top thirteen, that sooner or later the whole male and female population of the suburb will find its way into his files, every man a potential prowler, every female a victim. And what then?

19

In the middle of the last century in Rome, the old stone prison of the Mammertine on the Capitoline Hill, where St Peter is said to have been jailed, was set up as an oratory. Here, among the usual votive offerings, silver hearts, limbs, eyes with little filagree bows and angels about them, symbols of a miraculous return to wholeness, hung offerings of another sort: knives, meat-cleavers, clubs still wet from the skulls they had broken, and damp hair sticking to them, cords that had been used in a strangling, a dirty pillow, a pair of blood-stained scissors. The whole place, one writer tells us, was haunted; as if all the city's murders had gathered there and hung about, palpably, in the dark. Blood and the odour of blood had seeped into the stones. The air was thick with unspoken confessions and pleas for absolution. Within the city, a temple had been dedicated to the city's secret crimes. The criminals had crept away, but the instruments they had used were left to speak for them in a language, at once concrete and abstract, that made the whole place a whispering hall for abominable declarations, where the guilty might come, under cover of dark, to relieve themselves of the tokens of their guilt . . .

20

Detective Inspector Pierce, who is surprisingly literate, has read of this place and begins to be haunted by it. He also has dreams in which he imagines himself to be a computer, softly whirring as the pieces tumble into place within him and the day's facts are fed in, some dark act committed in the streets of the suburb, a new face (victim or violator, it hardly matters which), a private fantasy brought to light at last and tucked away in the memory bank, which is his own head. His head is filled with the crimes, real and imaginary, of a whole suburb, it bursts with them, the violence calmly subdued in compulsive rituals or breaking out in savage bloodshed. He staggers up out of these dreams in a cold sweat, terrified of where he might have been and who might have seen him there.

Often when Senior Detective Pierce has these dreams he is awake.

What frightens him most is that he has begun to

predict the crimes: the time, the place, the kind of woman. Has his accumulation of so much information, his entry into the pattern that lies under the facts, given him insight – unconscious as yet, but accurate – into the real nature of the crimes, so that a part of what is still to occur becomes visible to him? Does he begin to have so godlike a knowledge of us all that every detail of what we will, even those things that have not yet entered our heads and become the focus of will, is already clear to him? Or is there some simpler and more sinister explanation?

Senior Detective Pierce has asked twice now to be relieved of his duties and sent back to the Vice Squad, but on both occasions his request was refused.

Why? he wonders.

Is it because they have their eye on me and want to keep me where I can be watched? Even these notes are a dead give-away. I know too much. I have become a primary suspect.

Confess! Confess!